T0149574

The Bad Boy
and his French Maids

A sissy maid missy bad boy series, part one

m missy

authorHOUSE®

AuthorHouse™
1663 Liberty Drive
Bloomington, IN 47403
www.authorhouse.com
Phone: 1-800-839-8640

Published by AuthorHouse 3/26/2012

ISBN: 978-1-4685-6671-0 (sc)
ISBN: 978-1-4685-7201-8 (e)

INTRODUCTION:

Hello, my name is Morton and this is my story.

I grew up in southwestern Florida just outside of Naples. My twin sister, Mindy, and I were the only children of wealthy parents. We lived in a big house on approximately 10 acres of woods. The house was about 8000 square feet and had a nice pool with waterfalls, a hot tub, and even a diving board.

At 18 years of age I had the most perfect life I could ever imagine. I was the best tennis player in my high school and maybe in the county. My parents sent me to tennis camp every summer and I had lessons throughout the year as well.

I was a great baseball player, especially an outfielder that Willy Mays would be proud. I lead the team with on base percentage and led the league in walks every year.

My twin sister, Mindy, had the same opportunities that I had and was also an excellent tennis player, she did not play baseball.

We had all the money in the world as my father apparently made a great living and was very rich. So we never had any concerns that many of the other kids our

age had. We Both got new cars for our 18th birthday and I should tell you that I became a point of jealousy from the other kids as I drove a $90,000.00 Jaguar. My sister chose a mustang and the other kids seemed to be ok with that choice.

We both got excellent grades in school without much effort and were both considered to be some of the smartest kids in the school. I was sort of the king of the school as I was very popular and most everyone would follow me with any of my opinions.

Discipline was never a real problem as neither my sister or I ever got into any trouble. We did not even have to help clean the house as our parents had a live in maid.

However, my father graduated near the top of his class at West Point and became an army officer, before he became a business man. So, he had little patience for bad behavior. He taught my sister and me at an early age that you follow the rules or you get punished, Period. My dad use to tell me that was the way of the world and I may as well learn it when I was young enough to adjust to expectations.

My dad made the rules very clear in advance so there was never any surprises. My Father taught us his ten commandments of life, as my father called them.

One, always be obedient to those you need to obey.

Two, Always be polite, to everyone, all the time, no matter what.

Three, Always be friendly and nice to everyone, all the time.

Four, Always do the right thing, even when it's hard.

Five, Always be generous.

Six, There is no good reason to drink.

Seven, There is no good reason to smoke.

Eight, There is no good reason to take drugs.

Nine, There is not good reason to gamble.

Ten, always be honest with yourself and others.

Mindy and I learned and followed my Father's 10 commandments of life, most of the time, and were both very happy kids. Every time we were punished, it was because we forgot one of those rules.

From the time we were around 6 years old, if we were naughty, my dad would spank us with his hand over his knees and make us stand in the corner. After we turned 10, we would get our spankings, which were very rare, with a hardwood hairbrush. That was never something to look forward to.

Overall, over my 10 years of corporal punishment, from being six years old to 10 years old, I was probably spanked 6 times with my dad's hand. That's only 6 times in 4 years, so I was pretty good. My sister was probably spanked only 3 or 4 times.

From age 10 to 13 for me, I was spanked with the hairbrush only twice, that was twice too many for me. My sister, maybe three times.

From age 13 to 17 I did not enjoy my father's spanking brush about 5 times. I did seem to have a little problem as I went thru puberty and got three spankings that one year. Only one before and one after that middle year. My sister I think only got one more hairbrush spanking when she was 14 and that was it for her.

A spanking from our father was a sure and very unhappy event. Our father believed in two things when it came to a spanking. One, it should hurt more than enough for you ever to think that disobedience is worth the risk again. Two, it should be as embarrassing as possible as that sometimes was worse than the spanking.

Therefore, a spanking in our house was always a public affair. In other words Mindy or me would be spanked in the living room and whichever child was not being spanked was there to watch the one who was getting the spanking.

Additionally, my mother was there, but the worst part was that the maid, Sabrina, was there also. As Sabrina hated me, she never missed a good smile as she watched me get a spanking. I also noticed that when it was my sister turn to get spanked that Sabrina was not around.

As I said, our father made the spankings as embarrassing as possible. First he made us stand in the corner for about 30 minutes before each spanking, sort of advertizing to everyone else that a spanking was on its way.

Then right there in front of everyone, our father would call us to his side, as he sat on the spanking chair, and lower my pants and underwear. In my sister case, it most likely was lowering her panties and flipping her skirt up over her back, but you get the idea.

The end result was that you had your naked butt out there for everyone to see. In my case everyone got to see my penis also which was almost the most embarrassing part. This got worse in my later years as I would also get an erection. So for the last 4 or 5 spankings of my life from my father I had to stand there in front of everyone, especially Sabrina, with an erection.

Now, I had no idea at this point in my life what the erection was all about as I could not see where they were any good for anything, but for some reason, I felt embarrassed that I had one.

For some reason also, for the last two spankings that my sister Mindy got I also got an erection watching her get her ass bared and especially as it was spanked over my dad's lap and Mindy wiggled it all over the place and my dad spanked her so hard and for so long.

I loved watching Mindy's ass turn all red, then dark red, then sort of purple, and then some black and blue. Before my father stopped spanking Mindy my penis was throbbing for some unknown reason to me.

I think the part I liked the best was the crying. I really like to hear Mindy cry as the spanking went on and on and on. I liked it the best when Mindy cried so hard that I knew she had lost complete control of herself as the spanking was hurting her so much.

When I was the one getting the spanking, as I said, I was really embarrassed to have my ass bared in front of Mindy and Sabrina, not so much for my mother. In my later spankings, as I stood in the corner waiting for my spanking, I was worried about having an erection in front of Sabrina. I seemed to get an erection just from thinking about how embarrassed I would get later.

But, the worst part was when I started to cry, just like Mindy cried. I was so embarrassed to cry in front of Mindy, but especially in front of Sabrina. Nevertheless, no matter how hard I wanted not to cry, I could not stop myself as my dad spanked me so hard and for such a long time that I could do nothing but lay there over his lap and take my spanking and cry my eyes out.

Our dad believed that a spanking should be long enough and hard enough so that we remembered it for a long time. But, more importantly, he believed that the spanking should hurt so much and that you should be embarrassed so much that not taking any chances on ever getting another one was our goal.

Our father always met his goal as neither Mindy nor me ever would take a chance at doing anything that would result in getting a spanking. So, we only got a few, a few too many. But, they were rare and only for doing stupid things that for one reason of another we did not seem to stay out of as after all, we were young stupid kids in a way and made stupid mistakes.

After the spanking was over, we were sent back to the corner for another 30 minutes but I had to stand there without my pants or underwear so everyone one could

see my well spanked ass as I still cried for a while from both the pain and the embarrassment of having to stand in the corner showing off my spanked ass.

When it was Mindy's turn, she had to hold up the back of her skirt to show off her spanked ass. I loved sitting in the living room after Mindy got spanked and just look at her nice plump ass.

AS I got older I did realize that my embarrassment did not actually come all that much from the process of the spanking, the baring of my ass, the erection for all to see, the crying, but rather, I thought the most embarrassing part was that I was there to be spanked for being bad.

I always felt like a bad kid during those times and the embarrassment I felt from feeling like a bad kid was the part that bothered me the most.

Having told you all this, I do not want you to think that Mindy or me felt like our dad was cruel or mean in anyway. He spent most of his time playing with us, teaching us, and loving us.

Looking back on the growing years, we did not ever smoke, drink, sniff glue, take drugs, or do any of the other stupid things that many of our friends were doing. So, my dad's theory about spanking seemed to ring true and he kept us out of trouble by making us fear spankings.

THE STORY BEGINS:

However, this story, my story to you, starts when Mindy and I were 18 years old and my parents were killed when their own private plane crashed in Alaska when they were on vacation and got stuck in a sudden snow storm in early August of 2005.

Our parents left all of their assets to my sister and I in a trust fund which amounted to over 10 million dollars. My sister and I would get equal shares of the income from the trust until we were 25 years old and then we would be given our shares of the trust outright. The income amounted to about over 30,000.00 per month for each of us, after taxes.

Now, considering we lived in a fully paid 2 million dollar house we certainly did not need all that money to pay the household bills, so the trustee paid all our bills, gave us each an allowance, and allowed the trust amount to keep on growing.

However, as Mindy and me were just 18 years old, the trust required that we have an adult guardian live with us until we were 21 years old. It also required that we have a four year college degree by the time we were 25 in order to get the money from the trust.

Otherwise, we needed to wait until we 30 years old to get the money from the trust.

Our Mother requested within the trust that we take in her best friend, Molly, as our guardian, together with her twin daughters, Ally and Cally.

My sister and I agreed to honor our dead Mother's wishes and have Molly and her twin daughters come live in our house with Molly as our guardian. Molly really needed this break as she did not make very much money and her husband, who left her five years earlier, was not paying any child support.

As both my sister and I knew Molly and her two girls very well, it seemed to be a good fit for everyone as both my sister and I liked the three of them. Our only obligation under the trust fund was to have at least one guardian live with us as Mindy and I were under 21 at the time. So, this solution seemed to be an easy answer.

So life continued for me and my sister for the next several months, but it was different without our parents. I played a lot of tennis and baseball and continued to do well in school. I just missed my parents and cried myself to sleep on several nights.

CAST OF CHARACTORS:

MORTON:

My name is Morton, Mort for short and as I said I was 18 years old. Although I was a very good tennis player and baseball player, I was only five foot seven inches tall but was hoping to get taller in my later teenage years.

However, that may only be a hope and a prayer as my mom was only five foot tall and my dad was only five foot eight inches tall. No one in my mother's or father's family was much taller, so most likely I would end up being just be too short for my own liking.

In addition to being short, I was also small. I only weighed about 125 pounds and had a 27 inch waist line. The only place I seemed to have any muscles was in my ass and thighs. For some reason I had developed a nice size and nicely shaped ass and two large thighs.

However, my sister would tell me that I had such nice looking legs for a guy. Mindy called them "girly" legs. Some of her girl friends use to tease me about my "girly" legs as well, but it was all in fun, more fun for them than me, but it was alright.

I worked out a lot over the past few years hoping to build some muscles to make up for my small size and that seemed to help but it mostly just seemed to help maintain my thighs and nice ass. The bottom line here was that I was too small to ever really considering playing profession sports.

However, I also seem to be a good looking young fellow as I did not seem to have any problem attraction the attention of the girls. In fact, I was able to date almost any girl I wanted.

Apparently I was pretty smart also as I got almost straight "A"s in a Catholic school without much effort. Usually, I did not even have to study or do much homework, I heard the teacher explain something once and I just knew it.

I guess to be fair as I am going to tell you about the bodies of the females in this house, I should note the in addition to being short and skinny I also had a short penis. The poor thing was only about five inches long but it was pretty fat, not that that helps much, so I guess I will be no stud in the dating life as I get older. Maybe it will still grow some, but as with my height, that is just a hope and a prayer.

MINDY:

My Sister's name is Mindy, (yes, we are Mort and Mindy). Mindy was also very short, only five foot two inches tall, but she did have a nice set of full round tits and a nice plump ass. Mindy had long brown hair, a great smile, and was very nice looking. Mindy was also real smart and got good marks in school without much effort.

As with me and girls, Mindy did not seem to have any problems getting the attention of any male creatures and seemed to have her pick of any guy she wanted.

My Sister and I were real good friends and could discuss anything, even our sexual lives as they developed.

MOLLY:

My mother's best friend was Molly and she was about 38 years old and was five foot nine inches tall. Molly had medium length brown hair, small tits, nice sexy legs, and she had a nice full round ass. Molly also had a nice smile and still had a young looking face.

Molly was the mother of the twins, Ally and Cally. Molly and our mother were married on the same day and had their twins on the same day. What are the chances of that happening?

Molly and her two daughters lived in a two bedroom apartment which was not in an very nice neighborhood. So, coming to live in our huge home was like hitting the lottery for them.

Molly had a full time job, but she did not have a college education, so she did not make very much money and had no opportunity to do so in the future.

ALLY AND CALLY:

Molly's twin daughters names were Ally and Cally. Both Ally and Cally were about as tall as their mother even though they were only 18 years old also. Both Ally and Cally had long blond hair, nice smiles, and were very pretty.

Both Girls had nice long sexy legs like their mom, but unlike their mom they both had some nice firm round tits, not real big, but big enough to have a nice figure. They also both had nice plump asses to go along with those nice legs.

I think if I did not know both of them for all of our lives and were not friends that I would have loved to fuck both of them.

Aside from their good looks and great bodies, However, Ally seemed angry and rebellious, unhappy. Ally dressed like a slob and always seemed unhappy.

Cally, Well, there was something about Cally. Cally, seemed special somehow, Cally seemed extra smart, Cally carried herself like a real lady. Cally walked, talked, sat, and even stood differently, very sexy. Additionally, there was something else, something that I have never seen in any girl or a even in any lady before, something that I could not describe, There was just something real special about Cally.

Sabrina was my parents live in maid. I note that she was my parents maid as she did not seem to pay much attention to my needs or my room and this created a growing conflict between Sabrina and me for a number of years prior to this year.

Sabrina was about 26 years old and is a mixture of a South American Indian and black. The result made Sabrina very tall, about six foot tall, a good looking Indian with darker skin then an American Indian but not dark enough to look black.

Sabrina had very nice long and very sexy legs, a real nice muscular looking ass, medium sized tits, big enough to give her a nice figure, but nothing to say wow about. Sabrina also had a nice smile and very nice very long black hair.

I would have gotten rid of Sabrina after the funeral, but in my Moms will she asked that we keep Sabrina. Sabrina had kept my mother happy for many years since Sabrina came to be the maid when she was only 18, about 8 years ago.

I would have gotten rid of Sabrina because even though my Mom acted like Sabrina was part of the family, the fact was that Sabrina was a lousy maid. I use to complain about her all the time and the more I had to say the less

and less service I got. It was like Sabrina would punish me for trying to get her to do her job better.

Anyway, my mom and Sabrina were like best friends, so there was not much I could do, no one seemed to care about what I had to say when it came to Sabrina. Even now, my mom, was reaching back from the grave to try and protect Sabrina from me.

I loved my mom so much and we had such a great friendly and loving relationship, that I could not dismiss her request and agreed with my sister, Mindy, to keep Sabrina on, at least for a while to see if she would shape up. After all, I was now the Boss of the house, she would obey me now, NO?

LIFE MOVED ON:

ALLY:

As life moved on for me over the month or so, the first thing I noticed was that I was living in a house with five other females, three of which were very pretty 18 year old girls. Even Sabrina was a real nice looking young women.

However, except for my sister, I was the shortest and youngest person in the house so I had to look up to everyone, so to speak. Especially Sabrina, when she would wear high heels she could be as much as 9 inches taller than me.

The first thing that started to bother me was Ally. Ally had some attitude about her and she was not even polite enough to say hello or good morning or good evening or anything. Ally thought that making a mean face at me was her way of saying hello.

Ally would not talk to me and did not seem to understand that she was living in my house and she should be grateful for the privilege. Instead Ally acted like she

was angry because I had such a nice house and plenty of money and she had nothing.

Ally's lack of common respect was bad enough and it got to the point where I just ignored her also. However, Ally was a slob also and that was more of a problem for me. Ally's room was closer to the center of the house and mine was on the end of the house at the end of the hallway. So I needed to pass Ally's room to get to my room. Ally's room was nothing but a mess.

I think everything that Ally owned was on the floor. At least all of her clothes seemed to be on the floor. I even watched her looking for clothes to wear on occasion and she would look thru all the stuff on the floor until she found her bra, her panties, her skirt, her everything. How could she enjoy living like that I thought?

Regardless, I started to say something about the condition of her room and she had the nerve to look at me and tell me that I have a maid, have her clean it if I don't like it. I could not believe it and just walked away from her.

I went to see her mother, Molly, and discussed that matter with her. Molly told me that she would get Ally to clean her room. Ally would clean her room at that point, but that was only temporary as the next day she would start all over again leaving everything she used on the floor until it looked just that same.

Then Molly started having curfew problem with Ally. Ally was always suppose to be in by midnight and she started coming in later and later especially on the weekends.

Then there were grade problems with Ally as Molly told me that Ally never got great marks, but over the past six months her grades started to go down and she no longer got "B"s and "C"s but was getting C's and even some D's.

Then Ally started with "it's none of your business" when her mother wanted to know where she was going and who she was going there with. After a while, all Molly could get out of Ally about anything was, it's none of your business, this is my life!

Then there were other problems around the house. Ally would make a mess in the kitchen and leave it. All that was asked of her was to put her dirty stuff in the sink and Sabrina would take care of them, but even that was too much for Ally. Ally would just leave her dirty things on the table and that's if we were lucky. Many times she would eat in her room and leave the dirty things in her room to grow mold.

Once a week Ally was suppose to take any towels or sheets, or pillow cases, and dirty clothes from her room and bathroom and just put them in the hall outside her bedroom door. Sabrina would pick them up and wash and dry everything and bring them back for her. But, even that was too much trouble for Ally and her things were not getting cleaned to the point where her towels would begin to smell from mold growth.

CALLY:

Now, Cally, she seemed like the good girl when she first moved in. She always had a smile and said good morning, good afternoon, etc. Cally always kept her room clean, got good marks in school, was home on time, and cooperated with anything else I asked of her. Cally never had a smart mouth and seemed to always be in a good mood.

What happened to Cally I could not tell you, but she started to go down the same path of behavior as Ally. I guess she saw how well it was working for Ally and decided she could be have the same way.

I did not understand any of this behavior stuff as I grew up rich with a full time maid and I could have behaved like a spoiled brat but I did not, I followed my Father's 10 commandments of life. I behaved better and was more polite and more friendly and easier to get along with then Ally and Cally or even Sabrina, so what their problem was I had no clue.

I think Molly tried to be a good mother, but it seemed to me that Molly's idea of being a good mother was to try and be friends with the girls instead of disciplining them.

Molly did try to ground the girls on occasion. But what I saw happening was that after a couple of days of punishment, Molly would either forget about it or the

girls would just ignored her and the punishment would just disappear.

I sort of understood Molly's position, as she had to work for a living and worked long hours and came tired, maybe too tired to be a good mom.

SABRINA:

Sabrina, now there was another growing problem for me. While my parents were alive, for many years Sabrina treated me like I was a little punk and maybe I was to her. Sabrina spoke to me like I was just an annoyance to her and she and ignored anything I wanted.

Sabrina did not clean my room very often nor very well. I did not think she cleaned the rest of the house all that well and took way too much time off as well. I made comments to her from time to time and even showed her dirty corners in the kitchen, for example, but Sabrina just gave me mean faces and ignored me.

I guess as my punishment for thinking she was not a good maid, she would not use fabric softener on my clothes or towels which made then hard and scratchy compared to all of my sister things that were nice and soft and smelled good too.

Sabrina got away with her contempt for me and her lack of good maid skills because my parents or should I say my mother really liked her. They seemed more like buddies, they even went shopping together.

I think that Sabrina use to hid my stuff or not clean the things that she knew that I needed by certain dates. For example, she knew that I needed my baseball uniform on certain days and sometimes I could not find it or she would not have cleaned at all.

Sabrina would do the same thing with my white tennis shorts, sometimes she just did not get around to washing them and I would run out, especially on weekends if I played in tournaments and needed to play twice a day and needed two sets of clothes on a Friday, Saturday, and Sunday.

Now, I know that I was a young rich punk to her, but from my point of view she was the instigator of the problems. I just expected her to be a good maid and she seemed to think that as long as she was a friend to my mom that my mom would protect her and it turned out Sabrina was right, even in my mom's will my mom was trying to protect Sabrina.

However, now with my parents gone I thought that Sabrina would know that she needed to shape up or I would replace her. I thought that now that I was Sabrina's boss that she would show me the same respect that she showed to my mom.

But, no, Sabrina thought life would continue as before. But, Sabrina was wrong. Sabrina was so much more wrong then either of us could even have thought was possible at the time.

As I said, I would have gotten rid of Sabrina right after the funeral if it were not for Mindy asking me to give her a chance out of respect to our Mother, how could I say no? As it turned out we did keep Sabrina and that decision shaped the rest of my life. Maybe it was the worst decision on my entire life.

MOLLY, ALLY, CALLY AND I MEET:

As a result of all the problems that Molly was having with Ally and now Cally, I had a long chat with Molly and we agreed that both Ally and Cally would be transferred to the Catholic high school that my sister and I go too. Of course, I volunteered to pay for the tuition.

So as October approached the two girls, which were not happy about the decision to send them to Catholic school, had a long sit down meeting with Molly and me. They were told that their behavior needed to improve and, their marks needed to improve.

Ally and Cally were both told that no mark under a "C" was acceptable.

Ally and Cally were told that from now on that my Fathers 10 commandments of life would be posted in each of their rooms and that they would need to follow each and every rule as long as they lived in my house.

They were also told about how they needed to keep their rooms cleaned and had to be home by midnight, even on the weekends, unless other permission was granted.

I use to always say, nothing good ever happens after midnight. There are so many drunk drivers, crimes, car crashes, rapes, drug problems, etc. after midnight it was not all that safe to be out that late. There was also nothing to do after midnight that you could not do before midnight.

So, Ally and Cally were told that any breach of any of these rules would result in a punishment of my choosing, Period, end of story.

One, always be obedient, to those you need to obey.

Two, Always be polite, to everyone, all the time, no Matter what.

Three, Always be friendly and nice to everyone, all the time.

Four, Always do the right thing, even when it's hard.

Five, Always be generous.

Six, There is no good reason to drink.

Seven, There is no good reason to smoke.

Eight, There is no good reason to take drugs.

Nine, There is not good reason to gamble.

Ten, always be honest with yourself and others.

Ally, as I suspected, started with the mouth. This is so

unfair, all my friends go to the other school, he has a maid why do I have to clean anything, and so what if I get "D"s I was not planning on going to college anyway?

I told Ally that this was real simple and she was just trying to complicate her life. The bottom line here is that this is my house. In my house, you will behave the way you are told to behave, or you will move from my house, period, no discussion.

However, keep in mind, Ally, if and when you get kicked out, your sister and your mother don't get kicked out with you. So, we are not sure how you would support yourself.

The bottom line here, Ally, is that my parents taught my sister and me that if you make good decisions life, it will be better for you. If you make bad decisions, life will usually punish you. If you continue to make bad decisions, life will gang up on you and you will not be a happy person.

Ally, before you start thinking about how far you can push me, starting tomorrow any problems you cause will result in you getting a spanking. WHAT? Ally asked? as she got upset. Mom never spanks us!

That's right Ally, you mom never spanked you before and your mom will not be spanking you in the future. As I said, this is my house and I will be the one spanking you. Ally started to say something, or even yell something, but I held my hand up and said that's enough, you have been warned.

Cally said nothing but looked at me with this strange face

that I had not seen before, almost like she was trying to decide if I was buffing or not. Molly said nothing more and we told the girls that they were dismissed.

Molly told me afterwards that she knows that she agreed to allow spankings but now she was having second thoughts. I reminded Molly that nothing she had tried has worked so far and neither of the girls were going in the right direction. Molly just said, Yea, you're right, we'll see.

Now, as it looked like I was going to get to spank Ally and maybe Cally too, I went to the internet and did some research by looking up a few sites and found a hard wood hairbrush that would be good for giving that ungrateful child a good hard spanking.

Yea, I thought, that will straighten Ally's ass out and she will learn to behave and obey me around here and in general just become an agreeable person to live together in the same house.

A few days later the brush showed up in the mail and I just waited until that Ally bitch opened her mouth again to me. That night I was thinking that I was anxious to use my new hairbrush so I decided to try and move the timeline up to as soon as possible.

I started to think more and more about having Ally's bare butt over my lap and spanking the daylights out of her with that hairbrush. Those thoughts would produce a iron like, hard cock, every time I thought about it.

SPANKING ALLY:

Three days later the spanking brush arrived, the first week in October. I went right home after school as I was excited to see the new spanking brush. I get home about 40 minutes before Ally as I have no last period in school as she does.

I waited for Ally to get home and when I heard her in her room I went into her room and again started to complain how messy it was and that this is my house and she will obey me and keep her room clean all the time, everyday!

Ally flew back at me with, SO WHAT? This is my room so just get out and leave me alone. I guess Ally did not take the warning about getting a spanking to seriously and that was working out well for me as I wanted to spank her so bad at this point in time.

I went back to my room and got the hairbrush off my dresser and came back to her room. I waived the hairbrush at her and told Ally that she was warned about her mouth and her room and that she needed a good old fashion spanking to teach her some manners.

Ally started screaming for her mom and at the same time I went to her and grabbed her by her arm and

pulled her over to the desk chair where I sat down and tried to drag Ally over my knees when her screaming produced her mom her the bedroom door.

Ally's mom looked at me and was ready to say something, but I guess she realized that she had already agreed to this and although Molly was skeptical, she knew she had no leverage. Molly knew I could always get another adult to move in here, even if we paid a guardian for the three years until we were 21.

So, with tears in her eyes, Molly told Ally to cooperate with me unless she wanted to move out on her own and support herself somehow. Otherwise Ally, you have no choice in the matter, if you want to stay here. Ally, I suggest you cooperate with Mort and take your spanking and then learn to be a good girl.

Ally started to yell at her mom, you cannot be serious, you cannot let him spank me!!!!!!!!!!! Ally's mom asked her if she wanted to move out? Ally said, no fucking way, what a mouth on this kid I thought. Well then Ally, Molly said, I guess you will need to learn to obey Mort then. There does not seem to be anything I can do about it, now it's up to you.

I can tell you one thing for sure Ally, and that is that Cally and I don't want to move out of here just because of you, so I guess I need to support Mort in this as I have tried everything I know to get you to understand and behave, but nothing has worked. Now Mort is going to try it his way.

As Ally became confused she relaxed a little and I was able to pull her over my lap, I flipped up her short

skirt and started to pull down her panties, when Ally's hand came back in an attempt to protect her panties. I just stopped and said, Ally, it's the panties or the front door.

Ally again looked over to her mom for help and Molly said nothing to help her. So, Ally, moved her hand back in front of her and put it on the floor and used it to support her weight while her legs on the other side barely touched the floor.

My cock was rock hard but I did not know if it was from having a nice ass over my lap to look at, as Ally had a real nice ass, or if it was because I was excited by the expectation of spanking Ally.

When I looked at this spanking stuff on the internet, when I bought the hairbrush, I did get excited by watching the videos of other girls getting spanked. But, then again, there was always a nice ass to look at also and I was a big fan of a nice looking asses.

Regardless, I pick up that real nice hardwood hairbrush and started to spank Ally's ass. Ally was already crying, she started crying when her panties came down, so I guessed Ally was crying from the embarrassment. For some reason, I seemed to like the fact that Ally was embarrassed.

I spanked Ally slowly and watched her ass cheeks turn pink. Ally kicked her legs back one at a time and wiggled her nice ass all over my lap and against my hard cock. She even kicked her panties off that were resting just below her knees

Ally did not seem to be crying any louder as I continued to spank that nice ass, although I was having a real nice time watching her wiggle that fine ass all over for me. I also like watching it change colors as it was going from pink to a darker shade of red.

However, I wanted Ally to feel this spanking, I really wanted to hurt that ass and punish that ass, so I started to spank Ally harder and as I did Ally started to kick with more aggression and scream a little and cry even harder.

I thought that I was getting somewhere. So, I spanked even harder as Ally was turning her head from side to side and moaning and screaming and crying even harder.

As I spanked her harder and harder I also liked that fact that her ass was turning from dark red to more of a black and blue color, so I knew I was giving her a very painful spanking and that she was not faking me out by her screaming and crying. I figured I gave her about 50 to 70 spanks at this point and thought that was enough and I stopped.

I told Ally that she could get up and go and stand in the corner, but as I helped her get off my lap, she said "I am not going to stand in any fucking corner".

Before Ally knew what happened I push her back over my lap and flipped up her skirt again and started to spank her even harder and much faster than before while I told her to let me know when she's willing to obey me.

Instantly she started saying that she was sorry and she

will stand in the corner and she will obey me. I gave her another 25 or 30 spanks, maybe even 40 or so and stopped again. I asked, Ally, what did you say? Ally repeated that she will obey me, so I let her up again.

As Ally got off my lap I looked at her face and saw that her eyes were all red, her nose was clogged with snot and was dripping, and she was crying harder than ever, with her makeup running down her face.

I pointed to the corner I wanted her to stand in and she went right to it this time. Then I told her to hold up her skirt so that I could see her nice spanked ass. She made some groaning sound, as if she was really annoyed with me, but she did obey me.

I have no idea as to what Ally thought about that spanking or her time standing in the corner, but I loved it and I knew that this spanking was just the beginning, I knew I would be spanking that ass a lot in the future. I was the Boss of this house now and anyone who did not like it could get out or get spanked.

I left Ally there to stand in the corner and left, but before I got back to my room I realized that Ally was standing in the corner of her own room. I thought that it would be much more embarrassing for Ally if she stood in a corner where everyone could see her. So I turned around and went back and told Ally to follow me, Ally dropped her skirt and huffed a little, but obeyed me and followed me.

I took Ally down to the middle of the hallway and told her to stand in the corner there. Ally just looked at me with eyes that wanted to yell at me, but she controlled herself and obeyed me. The problem for Ally and the

benefit for me in making Ally stand in that corner is three fold;

First, it was a central part of the house at the top of the steps where everyone would need to pass to go to their rooms, so Ally would be on full display showing off her nice freshly spanked black and blue ass to anyone going by, which I thought would embarrass her more.

Second, there were mirrors on two sides of her so that not only could they see Ally holding up her skirt and showing off her spanked ass, they could see her face thru the mirrors which showed that she had been crying as all her makeup was running down her face.

Third, if someone came in the front door, they could also see Ally standing in that corner as well. So, Ally had to worry the whole time that no one came to the front door.

I thought these three benefits were much more humiliating for Ally and therefore more fun for me, but it also sent a message to everyone else in that house that they better be careful or they may be next.

Regardless, I was hoping that they all got a turn, I wanted to spank the daylights out of all of them. Well, that was not really true, I had no reason to want to spank my sister Mindy.

I let Ally stand there in the corner for about 30 minutes and then I told her she could go put her panties back on. However, Ally, I also want you to gather up my sister, your sister, your mother, and even the maid and meet me in the living room in 15 minutes.

FAMILY MEETING:

I asked Molly to gather everyone in the living room after dinner so we could chat. When I got to the living room 15 minutes later they were all waiting for me. I told my sister to sit next to me and for the other four to sit across from us.

I reminded the four of them, Molly the mother, Ally and Cally the twin daughters, and the maid that this house belongs to my sister and I and not them. That they were only invited to live there as we needed at least one adult to live with us and they were lucky we chose them as we could have chosen anybody we wanted.

We could have even hired a nurse to live with us. As I was telling them all of this, I, myself, started to wonder why we could not have use Sabrina as the adult. Was it only because of my moms' wishes or was there another reason that Sabrina could not be our adult? Something I was going to look into.

I reminded them that they always have the choice, you can go and find somewhere else to live or you can behave and be polite and be respectful and most importantly, you need to obey us. I told Ally to stand up and turn around and lower her panties and show everyone her

spanked ass. Again, Ally looked at her mom and her mom pushed her on the shoulder and told her to do it.

As Ally showed everyone her well spanked ass, they all went AHH!!!!! Alright Ally, pull up your panties and sit back down. I continued to tell everyone that from now on the my sister and I will be in charge of this house and anybody who does not do what they are told can either leave and go live somewhere else or they can be punished like Ally just was until they learn their place.

Everyone understand? They all just looked in shock. So I told them from now on they respond to me with yes Sir, no sir and to my sister as yes Miss, or no Miss. Now, everyone understand? Now I heard yes Sir, from everyone. However, I added, that rule does not apply to Molly as she may use our first names as she is the adult of the house.

My sister never really had a problem with any of their attitudes but then she did not care about what I wanted to do either. So, all the changes were basically up to me as Mindy did not intend to spank anybody. Mindy, however, was not objecting to what I wanted to do and gave me her support.

Later that evening, Molly came to see me when I was watching TV and told me that I was not wrong. Molly told me that her daughters grew up poor and without a father for the past 5 years to provide any male guidance and that they do need to learn to be more polite and respectful, but that they saw me as just another kid as I am only 18 myself.

Molly told me that Ally would be the real challenge and

that Cally should be much easier to handle as Cally did not seem to have the same bad mouth or angry attitude that Ally has. Molly said that Cally even use to get real good marks in school, that it was only in the past six months that her marks have fallen off.

I explained to Molly that I did not think that keeping ones room clean and saying good morning or good evening to someone that you pass in the hallway was too much to expect from someone you share a house with instead of making faces at them and ignoring them when they may speak to you. Molly again said that she understood and would work with me.

Over the next week or so both Ally and Cally were more polite and would say good morning or hello when they came home from school and their rooms were cleaner. Cally did a nice job, but Ally was not as neat as I would like her room to be, but it was a start. I realized that my idea of clean and theirs were nowhere near the same.

THE THREE FATIES:

As I told you before I always got great marks and was a good tennis player and a good baseball player, so I was pretty popular with all the "jocks" in the school. I was also very popular with the girls and could get a date easily at any time with almost any girl I chose. I also never got into any trouble in school or had any enemies either.

Well, there was these three fat girls that would hang around together all the time. I really never teased them about being fat pigs or made a mention of it at all. I never picked on anybody or had a bad word to say about anybody.

If I had a problem with anyone, I would just keep it to myself. But, this day, for some reason that I could not explain I was talking to some of other kids and I spoke to them about the three fat girls and called them the "THREE FATIES".

From that day one everyone in school called them the three fatties and not in a nice way. One day I found out that one of the three fatties found out that I was the one who started the three fatties name and told the other kid that her brother was going to beat me up.

Well, that did not sound like a good idea to me, after all, I was the Boss of my home and the king of the school. No one was going to beat me up! So, I hired this big kid to go and beat him up first and warn him if anyone beat me up that he would be back to beat him up again.

Needless to say, I did not get beat up. But, I did gain a few enemies because of the fatties name. I never did anything like that before, but now that I did, I thought it was fun.

More importantly, for me at the time, this increased my thoughts of being the Boss or king of the school. I felt even more powerful as I could control people now and I was liking it. I could punish those in my house and now I was able to have the kid that wanted to beat me up punished as well. Life was getting better all the time for me.

ALLY AND THE SPANKING BRUSH AGAIN:

However it was only two weeks after Ally's spanking that her room seemed to get more messy every day. Ally either did not care about what I had expected or she was testing me. I thought about it and decided to warn her one more time.

That evening I walked past her room when she was in there doing her homework and told Ally that I was not kidding about keeping you room clean and that means every day, not once a month.

I was surprised when Ally responded to me with "who died and left you boss" I thought to myself that my mom and dad died and left me boss, but I really did not think that she was really being personal, rather Ally was using that line in the generic sense, otherwise I would really have been angry instead of just feeling disrespected.

Regardless, I told Ally to get up and go stand in the corner. Ally, just sat there and made mean faces at me. Ally, I said, go and stand in the corner and do it now! Ally stomped out of her room and went to find her mom

instead of obeying me. About 10 minutes later Ally was standing in the corner in the 2nd floor hallway where I wanted her.

I did not know if Ally thought she was getting away with just standing in the corner or if she knew that she was going to get another spanking. But, I knew that I was going to give her another spanking and I intended it to much more memorable then the last one, which she apparently has forgotten about in just over two weeks.

I was remembering what my dad use to tell Mindy and I, that light punishments are soon forgotten. Apparently I was too easy on Ally when I spanked her last time, a mistake I did not intend to repeat.

I went down to Cally's room and told her to get her mother and the maid and to meet me in the living room in 30 minutes. I went to my sisters room and told her that I was going to spank Ally again and asked her if she wanted to watch.

Why she asked? Because I thought that it would be more embarrassing for Ally and that would add to her punishment and maybe she would remember it longer than two weeks. I reminded Mindy of how dad use to use our embarrassment against us. Mindy, looked at me and told me that she did remember, so alright, I'll come along.

When I got to the living room 30 minutes later Cally, Molly, and Sabrina were all there. I told the Sabrina to get a straight backed chair from the dining room and put it in the middle of the floor.

Sabrina looked at me and said, can't you get it yourself, you are closer to the dining room? I did not respond to Sabrina and went to the dining room and got the chair myself. I was sure that Sabrina was proud of herself, at least for the time being.

I put the chair down in the middle of the floor and put the hairbrush on the seat and turned around to see up over the railing to the second floor where Ally was standing in the corner and told her to come down. She stomped down the steps and stood next to me with her sour puss, you got to be kidding me face.

I was not going to back down from this challenge and I sat down on the chair and told her to come here and as she came over to my side, I reached up under her skirt and slid her panties down to her knees. I really expected more drama from Ally when I went after her panties, but I guess her mom already told her it was her own fault and it was my way or the front door way.

I took Ally's hand and guided her over my lap and flipped up the back of her skirt to rest on her back and took a few seconds to enjoy the view as Ally had one hell of an ass for a 18 year old girl. Then I started to spank her with my hairbrush about as hard as I could. Like last time, she started to kick her legs and kicked her panties half way across the room right away.

I decided that I was going to give Ally a longer and harder spanking to teach her that I am the Boss around here. I wanted the others to watch so they would know that I meant business and to embarrass Ally all the more at the same time.

I spanked the day lights out of that little bitch and made sure that I snapped my wrist after each and every spank to make sure it hurt the most it could. I really liked watching Ally's ass turn colors from the hairbrush, first red, then dark red and then sort of purple and then black and blue.

I liked how Ally would kick her legs and wiggle her ass all over my lap and against my rock hard cock, which felt very good even thru my pants. I kept up a steady spanking pace and enjoyed the hell out of listening to Ally cry. The harder Ally cried the more I liked it and that encouraged me to spank her even harder and even longer.

I looked over to all the others watching Ally get this spanking and they all looked somewhat scared themselves. I thought that was a good thing and picked one spot on Ally's ass and spanked it 15 to 20 times and then picked another spot and spanked it 15 to 20 times and so on and so on, spank after spank after spank.

When I got to about 200 total spanks and Ally was crying even louder I started to feel sorry for her and stopped spanking that real nice ass. When I stopped spanking Ally, she just drooped over my lap and cried and cried and cried even more.

I was hoping that she was getting the point that she needed to obey me, but on the other hand, if she did not learn her lesson I will get to spank her more and that was fine with me also. Either way I win, I thought. I either get obedience or I get to punish Ally, as I said, a win for me either way.

As Ally's crying died down I told her to get up and go back to the corner. I helped Ally to her feet and she went back upstairs and stood in the corner in the middle of the hallway where the mirrors were and where everybody could still see her.

Again, I had Ally hold up the back of her skirt so everyone could see what happens to asses around here if they don't obey the new Boss of this house. Good for me, I thought, for the first time in my life I has some authority and some power and I was liking it.

However, I was not finished with the spanking for today. I asked for everyone's attention again and I said, now that everyone knows that I will not put up with anymore disobedience around here you may have noticed that our maid, Sabrina, was told to get the chair I was sitting on and to put it here before I spanked Ally. You may have noticed that she disobeyed me and was also rude to me. Therefore, I will now spank her also.

Sabrina, jumped up from her seat and said, "there is no way in fucking hell that I am going to let anybody spank me, especially some little snot nosed kid that thinks he's a big deal because he has a lot of money!"

I guess Sabrina did not know the rule about, he who has the gold makes the rules? Sabrina, I said, I know a few things about you, First you are an illegal immigrant, second we pay you about 50% to 60% more then you can get anywhere else, and third you are not even a good maid.

Apparently because you are 7 years older them me and you got away with your poor work with my parents that think you can continue to do so. However, Sabrina, I have already warned you that I am the Boss around here and you will obey me or you will be punished or

you can go back to South America. So, Sabrina, you either get over here and get your spanking, or I can call immigration. Which will it be Sabrina? I asked?

With fuming anger in her eyes Sabrina came over to me to get her spanking. Sabrina had a longer dress on then Ally and I could not reach up under it to remove her panties so I told Sabrina to lift her dress, as she did I was able to lower her panties and told her to get over my lap.

I was extra thrilled to be able to spank Sabrina because of the way she has treated me so poorly for the last 7 years. I was also really liking the power I now had. I was going to teach that bitch, Sabrina, that she will obey me from now on or she will get punished by me, or she will get deported.

Sabrina laid over my lap and I flipped her dress up over her back uncovering her beautiful ass. I always thought Sabrina had a nice ass, but now I was getting to see it and I was not disappointed.

Ally's ass was more plump and more of a square shape, to me, the nicest ass a girl could have. Sabrina's ass was more narrow on the sides but was more muscular up and down and stuck up a little more. Different than Ally's but still a first class ass.

I did not spank Sabrina as hard or as long as I spanked Ally as it was the first time. However, like with Ally I thought that I would get a lot of chances in the future as they had those types of spirits that would continue to challenge me until I beat the obedience into them and I was looking forward to doing just that.

I gave Sabrina about 20 good spanks with the hairbrush before she kicked her panties off that I left resting around her knees. Sabrina was not crying like Ally and I could tell that she was fighting giving into the spanking. Maybe she was trying to tell me that I was not hurting her with her spanking, or maybe she was just older and could take more pain then Ally.

All the same with me, Sabrina was not getting off my lap and this spanking was not going to end until Sabrina was in tears. After all, I could not let her make any statement in front of the others that she was not being punished.

As the spanking approached 40 to 50 spanks I could tell the her resistance was wearing her down as she was kicking her legs more and moaning more loudly and groaning a lot more. Finally at about 60 spanks or so Sabrina lost her battle and broke out in tears.

I noticed, however, that I was not enjoying the color in Sabrina's ass as much as I did with Ally. With Ally, her bright white ass colored up real fast and real bright. Sabrina, having the darker skin, the spank marks did not show the color as well.

I did not get the pink color at all, nor much red. Instead Sabrina's ass just sort of turned a darker shade of the same color. Nevertheless, I enjoyed spanking Sabrina, even more the Ally, because of our history over the years, but I did miss the more colorful spanked ass cheeks.

I started to spank Sabrina a little harder and little faster and as I did she could not hold out any longer and really started to cry real hard. The harder I spanked Sabrina the harder she cried and I was loving it.

I was loving each and every spank, spank, spank, spank, spank! This was great I thought, I can't wait to spank the rest of those bitches as well. Well, I guess that is not a fair statement, as the only one left is Cally and Cally is no bitch.

I stopped spanking Sabrina with about 125 total spanks and allowed her to cry over my lap for a minute. When Sabrina pretty much stopped her crying and I sent her off to stand in the corner next to Ally.

I let the two spanked asses stand in the corner for about 30 minutes and told them that they were dismissed.

I went to the internet and looked up maid uniforms and found a bunch of sexy French maid uniforms and ordered five different ones. Wait until Sabrina finds out about what she is going to be wearing from now on I thought, I smiled to myself, but I also got a hard on.

I also bought some leather cuffs with D rings that could go on wrists or ankles. I bought a couple of rattan canes, one thick one and one thin one. The site said that the thin one does not hurt as much. I also bought a thick leather strap and a 12 foot long thin black whip.

I also bought a long rope that had a hook on one end so you could hook the rope to the cuffs and tie the other end to anything, like a tree. My cock got all hard just thinking about using these items to keep my flock of bitches in line. I found that both strange and exciting. The last thing I bought were five inch high heels, I bought two pairs, one in white and one in black.

SABRINA AND THE WHIP:

The following week all of the new clothes that I bought for Sabrina, as well as, all my other new toys showed up at the front door. After taking them all to my room and looking thru everything I decided today was a good day to get that maid, Sabrina, otherwise known by me as, the bitch, to begin wearing her new uniforms.

I picked out a nice black and white French maid dress, complete with a nice white satin apron, a pair of white stockings, white 5 inch high heels, and even a pair of white satin panties.

I took the stuff down to the maids room and then went to find Sabrina. I told Sabrina to follow me to her room. She did, But she did not say yes Sir. When we got to her room I showed her the French maid uniform and told he to put it on.

I expected to get a mean face and some under her breath grumbling and then obedience. After all, I had to assume that if Sabrina did not obey me, that she knew another spanking was going to forthcoming. However, what I got from Sabrina was, if you think I am going to wear that slut dress and that other crap you must be fucking nuts!!!!!!!

I said nothing and just walked away and went back to my room. Sabrina just gave me a reason to take her out back, tie her up to a tree and give her a good old fashion whipping, just like she was an old time slave. Who does that Sabrina think she was to talk to me like that I thought.

Sabrina was going to learn her place around here or she was going back to South America. Although it was her choice, it really was not much of a choice as she needed to job and the money to support her aging mother and father back in South America.

So I was convinced that I could treat Sabrina anyway I wanted and she would have to accept it. After all, let's be realistic here, Sabrina does work for me and she should obey me anyway.

Wearing a uniform that I like in the house where no one outside the house would see her should be acceptable to her, even if it was a very sexy uniform. But, I guess it was not agreeable with Sabrina.

I went to my room and got the wrist cuffs, the whip, and the rope and went back to the kitchen. I told Sabrina to hold out her hands and she looked at me like I was nuts. I looked at Sabrina and I remained her that it's my way or immigrations way, choose.

I was happy she chose my way because I was really looking forward to giving that bitch a good whipping. However, she has not seen the whip yet so she does not know what I had in mind for her, most likely she thought that she was going to get another spanking.

I put the cuffs on her wrists and hooked them together in front of her and told her to follow me. I took her out back where I attached the rope hook to her wrist cuffs and threw the rope up over a big tree limb.

I pulled Sabrina up real tight so that her hands were way high up over her head so she had to stand on her toes. I also remembered Sabrina that she followed me like I told her, but she did not say yes Sir as she was suppose to, all the worse for her I thought.

I left her hanging there and went inside and got a pair of scissors and came back and started to cut all of Sabrina's clothes off of her. She started to kick around, but I warned her again that it's my way or the immigration way.

I reminded her that she was in enough trouble all ready and asked her if she want to make it worse? At that, Sabrina calmed down and stopped trying to kick me. I finished cutting off all of her clothes until she was completely naked.

This obviously was the first time I ever saw Sabrina naked. In fact, this was the first time I saw any girl naked and I like what I saw. As I had see before when I spanked Sabrina, she had a very nice muscular ass, but now I could see that she also had nice full round breasts, a flat tummy, and nice long sexy legs. Those legs are going to look really good in those 5 inch high heels I brought for her to wear.

After I finished cutting off her clothes I walked all the way around Sabrina to get a look at my first naked girl. I never saw a girls pussy before and could not see much

with all that hair Sabrina had down there, but for some reason, my eyes were attracted to that area.

I Gave her ass a good looking over in this standing position as opposed to the over my lap position or the standing in the corner position. I really liked Sabrina's ass, very nice.

I moved back around to Sabrina's front and had a nice stare at her tits. The first time I had seen real live tits that were not in a book or in the movies. Sabrina had a real nice body I thought. I wondered when I started having sex if all the girls would look this nice. My cock sure loved Sabrina's body as it was pulsating up a storm in my pants.

After I threw Sabrina's cut up clothes to the side and finished staring at her body, I left her hanging there again and went back inside. I went up to Sabrina's room and picked out all of the clothes that she wears around the house to clean and took them all back outside with me and dropped them in a pile in front of her.

Sabrina had this face that she wanted to kill me and maybe she did as she has gotten away with lazy and poor service around here for years and now this young punk is taking it all away from her. I told her that from now on that she will wear only what I approve that she wear around the house and nothing else, period!

I started to cut up all of her clothes right in front of her and she just huffed and puffed but said nothing. I was sure that she knew that it would do her no good to say anything. I was really enjoying my feeling of power over

that bitch as she had to just wait there, naked, in front of me while I destroyed all her clothes.

I took my time and had a good time making her more angry by the minute. I enjoy watching her hang there all naked and angry. I knew that Sabrina had to be really embarrassed to be naked, especially in front of me, this 18 year old punk in her eyes.

Her obvious embarrassment made it all the more enjoyable for me. My cock seemed to be enjoying Sabrina's embarrassment, but my cock was also looking forward to listening to the bitch scream as I whipped her.

I finished cutting up all of her clothes and just left them in one big pile that Sabrina could see. I went back in the house and got the whip, now the real fun starts I thought.

I came back a few minutes later and thought about not showing Sabrina the whip. But then I thought that it would be more fun to scare her first. So, I walked around to Sabrina's front and right in front of Sabrina's face I uncoiled the whip and told her, see this whip?

Well, I am going to whip you just like in the old days when slaves needed to learn to obey. I am going to enjoy the hell out of whipping you and listening to you scream as you have disrespected me way to long and today you will find out that I am not kidding about you obeying me.

I could tell that she wanted to say something that she knew I did not want to hear, but she held her tongue.

I also enjoyed that little bit of her suffering and her humiliation. At that I walked around behind her and CRACK! I was impressed from the sound as the whip lashed across her back and left an nice angry looking welt.

I waited for her to respond to the lash and she did by kicking one of legs backward as she lunged forward a bit. CRACK! Again she did the same and CRACK! I gave her another and she moaned pretty loud. CRACK! she moaned even louder. CRACK! she screamed a bit as she squirmed around.

Obviously this is the first time that I was whipping someone, but after I got the whip in the mail I did practice with it in my room when no one was home and gave a couple of pillows a good workout.

I think that I practiced enough to learn that the secret to handling a whip was not to drag the whip thru its path, but rather to snap your wrist and stop the whips handle thereby causing the whip to accelerate and causing the tip to snap against Sabrina's back.

CRACK!!!!!! CRACK!!!!!! CRACK!!!!! CRACK!!!!! I kept giving Sabrina one lash about every 15 seconds. I was taking my time as I wanted to see her reaction and I wanted to her to suffer after each and every lash. I wanted to hurt Sabrina, to punish Sabrina, to teach Sabrina to obey me, and show respect for me.

CRACK!!!! CRACK!!!! CRACK!!!! CRACK!!!! CRACK!!!! I had her moaning after each lash at this point but I was not going to be happy until she cannot control herself anymore and cries like a little girl. I stepped back and

to the side a little so that I could get the whip to cover more of Sabrina's back and could get a better snap across her back as well.

That made a big difference as she started huffing and puffing and yelling more with each lash. CRACK!!!!!!!!! CRACK!!!!!!! CRACK!!!!! CRACK!!!!!!!!! CRACK!!!!!!!!!! That was much better and I knew Sabrina could not hold out much longer as she was getting louder and louder and struggling more than ever after each lash.

I also knew that she did not want to cry and wanted me to think that she could take it and that I was not really hurting her or really punishing her. I guess Sabrina thought that that may cause me to lose interest and therefore she would win this battle of wits.

But, she was wrong, dead wrong, as she was not getting released until she could not control all the tears and I could tell that she felt punished and she was willing to confess that she will obey me from now on. So, Sabrina's attitude just motivated me to whip her even harder.

CRACK!!!!!!!!!!! CRACK!!!!!!!!!! CRACK!!!!!!!!! CRACK!!!!!!!! CRACK!!!!!!!! Now we were making progress as we approach about 30 lashes as I felt the tears should be coming shortly. So I CRACK!!!!! CRACK!!!!!!!!! CRACK!!!!!!!!! CRACK!!!!!!! CRACK!!!! CRACK!!!!!!!!!!!

I whipped Sabrina even harder and she lost control and gave me a real nice loud scream followed by a big bunch of tears as she started to cry uncontrollably. As Sabrina started to cry, I took a minute to see all the welts there were developing on Sabrina back.

Those welts looked like they hurt as they seemed to get bigger and bigger as the minutes ticked by. Some of the welts were also showing signs of becoming blood blisters instead of just big red welts.

The tears and the crying encouraged me to whip Sabrina even harder and CRACK!!!!! CRACK!!!!! CRACK!!!!! CRACK!!!! CRACK!!!!!! I did just that and whipped her even harder. I whipped that bitch so hard that she lost all fight in herself and was just hanging there by her wrist cuffs. Sabrina just took the whipping, the CRACK!!!!!! CRACK!!!!!!!!! CRACK!!!! CRACK!!!!!!!!!!!! CRACK!!!!!!!!!! of the whip.

After about 50 lashes, which took about 10 minutes to deliver, I stopped and walked around to face Sabrina and as I showed her the whip again, I asked Sabrina if she was now willing to obey me.

As she hung there crying so hard I knew she was not really able to talk, but she did shake her head yes, but that was not good enough for me and I walked around to her back again and CRACK!!!!!! CRACK! CRACK! CRACK! CRACK! CRACK!!!!! CRACK!!!!!!!!!! CRACK!!!!!!!! CRACK!!!!!! CRACK!!!!!!!!!! CRACK!!!!!!!! CRACK!!!!!!!!!! CRACK!!!!!!!!!!!!!!!!!!

After another 10 hard lashes I walked back around to face Sabrina and asked her again, are you ready to obey me, I did not hear your answer the first time. If anything, this time Sabrina was crying more hysterically, but she choked out a yes Sir. I was not sure that I had broken her spirit completely, but it was broken at least for now.

I left her hanging there for about 10 minutes while I

put the whip back in my room and got myself a glass of water. Whipping Sabrina made me thirsty.

I came back and told Sabrina that I was going to let some slack in the rope that was holding her hands and arms far above her head as she was still only able to stand on her toes. As I do, I told Sabrina, I want you to drop to your knees, yes Sir, Sabrina whispered, as she was still in a lot of pain and very worn out from the whipped.

I could tell that I had succeeded in hurting Sabrina. I could tell that I succeeded in punishing Sabrina. I could tell that the whipping took a lot of the fight out of Sabrina and I was thrilled as in addition to being effective, that was a lot of fun.

As Sabrina landed on her knees I held the rope tight enough so that she still had her hands and arms stretched above her head so that she was just resting on her knees on the ground. Although this did release much of the weight off of her arms she still could not go anywhere.

I unsnapped my shorts and lowered my zipper and let my pants drop to the ground around my ankles. Then I lowered my underwear to my ankles as well.

Sabrina's face was now level with my rock hard cock and I told her to suck it. She looked at me with some additional tears in her eyes and I just said I told you to suck it bitch, or do you need more of my whip before you will obey me?

I was not sure what to expect or exactly what Sabrina may do as I have never had a blow job before. In fact, I was still a virgin. But, I saw girls giving blow jobs on

the internet so I figured I would make Sabrina give me a blow job and see what I thought.

Sabrina opened her mouth and I move forward so that my cock could slid into the mouth and she started to suck my cock slowly and not very well, or so I thought. It still felt real good and since I was about to explode even before I thought of making her such my cock, it did not take much to get me to cum.

But, Hay! Sabrina will either get real good at sucking my cock or she will be punished a lot more, or she will be on her way back to South America. We will see which she chooses, my guess is cock sucking.

Anyway, Sabrina was providing a little bit of cock sucking pressure as she slid my cock in and out of her mouth and she bobbed her head up and down and BAM! I exploded in Sabrina's mouth, pulse after pulse after pulse of hot cum. Sabrina did not swallow all of my cum and some started to leak out of her mouth and drip down her chin.

When I was finished I pulled my cock from her mouth and walked away with my pants in my hand and went inside to clean up and get redressed.

When I came back, I walked around to see Sabrina's face and it was a mess with all her makeup smeared all over her face from the crying and the tears. Sabrina also had some cum dripping down her chin as well. I looked at Sabrina, but she just looked at the ground. I asked her if she was ready to wear what I tell her to wear or does she want to go back to South America. Yes Sir!

Sabrina, who's the Boss around here now? You are Sir. Sabrina, who will you obey around her now? You Sir. Are you sure Sabrina, or do you need to be whipped more first, Yes Sir, I am sure! Alright then Sabrina, we will see won't we? Sabrina did not answer me, but then that was not really a question.

I let Sabrina down and she almost feel to the ground but I caught her as she stumbled forward. Sabrina tried to move away from me as she was still stark naked and did not want me to touch her, but she did not seem to have the strength to be fussy.

I told Sabrina to go and get cleaned up and put on her new uniform and come and find me so that I could approve it before she goes back to work. While I was waiting for Sabrina to come and find me I looked up some information in the internet on how to suck a cock. I also found some information on curtseying and how to curtsey and printed that as well.

About 15 minutes later Sabrina had washed her face, fixed her makeup, put on her new uniform, and came to find me so I could approve of her new look. I looked at her and thought that maybe I was making a mistake as she looked so good and so sexy that I got an instant erection and wanted to fuck her right there and then.

Funny, I never thought about fucking her before now. Considering I still have never fucked any girl, I thought that was a strange thought that I had.

I gave Sabrina the information on how to curtsey and told her to read it and practice tonight and starting

tomorrow every time I give her an order she will say yes Sir and then curtsey to me.

I also told her that anytime she sees me she will also say good morning Sir, or good afternoon sir, or good evening sir, etc and follow with a nice curtsey. Understand? Yes Sir, was all she said, so maybe she was learning.

I gave Sabrina the information on how to suck a cock and told her to also read it and starting tomorrow she will practice every day on me until she can do everything in the instructions with ease. Understand Sabrina? Yes Sir, Sabrina choked out, but I knew she did not want to say YES to anything about sucking my cock tomorrow or any day.

For some reason, that fact that she was being forced to serve me in that way made it all that more exciting for me. I could feel that Sabrina was really embarrassed about agree to by my personal blow job maid, but her embarrassment seemed to add to my excitement.

Additionally, I seemed to really like the idea that she had no choice in the Matter. I felt the same way about punishing all of them, I loved the idea that they had no better choice than to obey me, it gave me such a feeling of power. I was the boss of this house and everybody was going to obey me!!!!! Life was getting better all the time for me!

Later that evening I was chatting with Mindy and she told me that she did not think that I should be making Sabrina give me blow jobs. Mindy also heard about the "the three fatties" and told me that I was not being nice.

Mindy added that I have always been such a good son and a good boy, but those two things are things that bad boys would do. I looked at Mindy and told her that I understood her opinion, but said nothing more about it.

I thought to myself that if the three fatties did not want to be teased then maybe they should not be so damn fat, so maybe I was encouraging them to look at themselves and lose some weight.

As far as Sabrina and the blow jobs were concerned. Why was it bad to have your maid provide the services that the employer wants? Sabrina can always leave if she does not like it.

These were my thoughts to justify my turn towards being a BAD BOY!

CALLY GETS A SPANKING:

Two weeks later, in early November, Ally was doing a better job with keeping her room clean and Sabrina was being more polite and responsive to my requirements and so far Cally has behaved much better just because we had that chat.

Cally always was polite and said good morning, good night, hello, have a nice day. Cally would even have a conversation with me or jump into a conversation between me and my sister or even with Molly.

Cally seemed to enjoy speaking with me. Besides my sister, Cally seemed to be the only one I knew that could have an intelligent conversation with me. That impressed me about Cally, as in spite of her marks in school, Cally seemed much smarter.

The only problem with Cally was cleaning her room. She was better at keeping her room cleaned when she first moved in but I guess Ally taught her differently.

One day I went to Cally's room after school and told Cally that her room was not acceptable and to go and stand in the corner. Cally looked at me as if she wanted to say something and then thought better of it and just said, yes Sir, and started to walk away.

Wait Cally, I told Cally, on her way to the corner, tell Sabrina to get the spanking chair and the spanking brush out and put them in the living room. Again, Cally looked at me like she wanted to say something and again she did not. Cally just said yes Sir, again, and went on her way to go and stand in the corner.

I went down to the living room about 30 minutes later and no one was around but I did not care as it was not my goal to humiliate Cally. Although, I did tell her to tell Sabrina about the spanking chair and the spanking brush to embarrass Cally. Otherwise, I only wanted to spank her to teach her to keep her room clean.

I wondered why I did not care about humiliating Cally like I liked to do so much with Sabrina and Ally? All I could think of was that Cally was a very nice kid and that she did not have the same resistant personally as did Sabrina or Ally.

Cally was more submissive and seemed to take direction easily without objection. Even when I told Cally to go and stand in the corner she did not mean face me, sure she hesitated for a few seconds, but she did obeyed me and she even said yes Sir.

I sat down on the spanking chair and called Cally to my side. Cally came down the stairs and come over right to where she needed to be. I looked up at her from my sitting position and she looked at me. Unlike Sabrina and Ally I did not see any defiance in Cally's eyes or on her face.

Cally even had some tears in her eyes already. I was sure that Cally felt embarrassed to be getting this

spanking but she was not objecting like Sabrina and Ally did. Rather Cally seemed resigned to the fact that she was going to get a spanking and she was just being obedient.

I used my hand to move up under Cally's skirt and used my fingers to gently lower Cally panties. As I did I saw a few more tears dripping down Cally's cheeks.

I was sure that this lovely 18 year old girl did not want me to be seeing any parts of her that a 18 year old boy should not be seeing. Yet, Cally, was completely obedient to me.

Since Cally had not received any pain yet, I had to assume that those tears were a reflection of her embarrassment to have me lowering her panties and the knowledge that I would soon be seeing her bare ass as well. Even though it was not my goal to embarrassed Cally, I knew it would still happen and my cock really seemed to like the idea.

Even without instruction from me, Cally laid herself over my lap and I heard a little whimper of a cry from her as she did. I hesitated before starting to spank Cally as I was loving looking at her fine ass.

As you know, Ally and Cally are identical twins, so they both have basically the same great looking ass so I knew what to expect with Cally as I had seen Ally's nice ass when I spanked her. However, for some reason, I thought that Cally's ass was just a little bit nicer, a little more plump I'd say. Maybe even a little more firm.

I started to spank Cally pretty hard but not as hard as I

could have and Cally started to kick her legs and kicked her panties off and they flew over my head.

Cally also started to cry right away and did not try to fight it like Sabrina and Ally did. Cally wiggled her fine ass all over my lap, but I did not feel like she was ever trying to jump or fall off like Sabrina and Ally did.

I spanked Cally with about 50 spanks, enough to cover her entire ass with a nice red color, but not hard enough to cause any deep black and blue marks. Cally just laid there like a good girl that was getting a spanking that she knew she deserved and maybe even wanted.

Cally cried the whole time, but never screamed or hollered. One could almost get the impression that Cally's crying was cleansing her soul, maybe it was.

I stopped spanking Cally and let her cry for a minute over my lap and then helped her up and was going to tell her to go back and stand in the corner when she surprise me by saying, "I am sorry I disobeyed you, Sir. I was in shock, but I went with the flow and I Thanked Cally. Then I sent her back to the corner for another 30 minutes.

Cally turned towards the stairs and I noticed that she did not make any attempt to find her panties that were laying on the floor. Cally just walked slowly up the stairs and without me saying a word she used her hands to hold the back of her skirt up to show off her freshly spanked ass cheeks just like I made Ally and Sabrina, even though I did not tell her to do the same.

I went to the kitchen and got an egg timer and brought

it back to Cally and set it for 25 minutes and placed it on the table next to Cally. I told her that that her punishment was over when the timer went off. Cally, looked at me with her tear stained face and said thank you Sir.

I looked at Cally and told her that I hope she can keep her room clean in the future. Cally, said, "yes Sir", I will. Cally was not kidding either, as her room was kept in perfect shape after that day. I never even needed to remind her, ever again.

Odd, I thought, I did not enjoy spanking Cally as much as I enjoyed spanking Ally and Sabrina. I did not seem to have the interest in hurting Cally like I did with Ally and Sabrina.

I did enjoy looking at Cally's ass, I loved that part. I enjoy watching Cally's ass turn all red and bounce around and wiggle all over my lap. But, I had no thirst to spank Cally any harder or longer than necessary to get my point across.

I also did not think that Cally did all that crying because of the pain I caused her with the spanking brush. I felt like it was much more emotional with Cally, not so much pain. After all, Cally started crying before I ever touched that brush to her fine ass.

MORE SCHOOL AND ME:

As my past seems to be my future, there were these three black boys on the football team. These three kids were the biggest three in the school and I had no problem with them at all. I did not even care that they were black kids, I had no problem with anyone being black, they were just other kids to me.

However, since I thought it was so much fun, based on the positive response I got from all my friends and other to my naming "the three fatties" I started referring to these kids as "the three blackies".

I noticed these three black boys were hanging around together every day at lunch and started calling them "the three blackies" As you can image they were not happy about it. The name seemed to stick however and I seemed to be happy with my ability to create labels and have them stick. However, now I had three more kids that hated me.

Yes, in just two months of this school year I seemed to have gone from the kid everyone loved, to the kid that most others loved, except the ones I named and some of their friends. But, still, that was a growing number. I did not seem to care, after all, I was the king of the school, so the hell with them.

A few day later my sister Mindy looked at me, shook her head in dissatisfaction with me, and said, "the three blackies" HUH! Mort, that's what bad boys get involved in. Once again, I did not respond to Mindy.

VIRGINS NO MORE:

It was November 7th and neither my sister nor I had had sex yet but that was about to change. One Friday night my sister came home from a date with this strange look on her face and this sly smile that I had never seen before.

I asked her how her date was and she blushed like I had never seen from her blush before. I smiled and asked her, did you have sex? Mindy, smiled and said yes.

I asked Mindy what it was like and she basically told me that for her it hurt, but was nice. Mindy told me that she wanted to do it more with Jim, her boyfriend.

So, that set me off on the path of having sex also. I picked out a girl the next day in school and decided that I would have sex with her the following weekend. Getting her to agree to have sex with me was much easier than I thought it would be.

I don't think I was her first as she seemed to have a better idea as to what to do then I did. I learned everything I knew, which was not much, from the internet. But, it was enough to get the task completed.

After that day, I was on a mission to bed down every girl

that I thought as cute or even was not cute, but had a nice body. I even thought about fucking Ally and Cally, but for some reason, that was just too close to home for me and I stayed away from them.

But, then there was Sabrina and my blow jobs. As I could get Sabrina to suck my cock for me anytime I wanted too, I did not have the need or desire to have a relationship just for sex. I thought that was a good thing for me, however.

Sabrina was getting to be a good cock sucker and I think that she has come to terms with the fact that if she wants to stay here then giving me blow jobs will be part of her job.

Later, I found out from Mindy that Ally also already had sex with a few different guys. But, apparently Cally was still a virgin. Cally, in spite of her good looks did not show much interest in the boys. Cally had one girl friend that she spent most of her time with.

REPORT CARDS:

Mid November, it was report card day and I was sitting on the couch in the living room after dinner looking thru the mail when Mindy came in and sat down next to me and asked me how things were going with Sabrina?

I told Mindy that Sabrina seems to be getting the idea that she now works for us and not mom any longer and that she will either serve us the way we wanted to be served or she would be punished, or she could leave, it is always up to her.

Yes, Mindy said, but you really enjoyed punishing Sabrina and having Sabrina give you those blow jobs and that could become a dangerous path for you, Mort! I agreed with Mindy that I was enjoying training Sabrina and that I especially enjoyed punishing her.

However, I did not think there was any downside for me, Mindy. Only two things can really happen I said, one, Sabrina can leave and then we did not dishonor moms wishes by getting rid of her. Two, she will become the useful and respectful maid that we should have.

Besides, Mindy, we have made a lot of progress, watch this. I called Sabrina and Sabrina came in from the kitchen and came right up to me and said, yes Sir, how

may I help you, curtsey. My sister smiled and I could see Sabrina blushing with embarrassment as acting like that for me is one thing, but in front of my sister I could tell that embarrassed Sabrina even more. I guess she was use to me, I thought.

However, I noticed right away that as soon as I could tell that Sabrina was embarrassed that I got an erection. For, some reason, I was finding that embarrassing others was exciting to me. Maybe, that was why I started naming the other kids in school, their embarrassment was a thrill to me?

I told Sabrina to go and get the spanking brush and in spite of the nervous look I got from Sabrina, as she obviously thought that she was going to get a spanking. Sabrina gave me a yes Sir, a polite curtsey and off she went to get the spanking brush.

My sister asked if I was going to spank Sabrina and I told her no, that I was wanted Sabrina to think that was getting a spanking to show you that she is now overcoming herself and is now obeying much better, so, Mindy, maybe there is hope for Sabrina after all.

However, I told Mindy that I thought that someone was going to get a spanking after we check out the report cards of the two girls. What, Mindy asked? Remember Mindy, I told the girls that anything less than a "C" is not acceptable and that they would get a spanking for every mark lower that a "C" beginning this marking period. Since reports cards were given out yesterday and neither of the girls has volunteered a look, they must be worried.

Sabrina came back with the spanking brush and held it out for me to take as she asked if there was anything else she could do for me, curtsey. I told her to go and get the spanking chair and set it up in the middle of the room in its usual place, yes Sir, curtsey.

Sabrina blushed again in front of my sister. Sabrina's face was showing her embarrassment as she was still thinking that she may be the one to get a spanking. My cock was still hard and was enjoying Sabrina's embarrassment even more this time

When Sabrina came back with the chair, I told her to go and get Ally and Cally and tell them to bring their report cards with them, yes Sir, curtsey.

My sister and I chatted about a few other things while we waited. Mindy and I had a great relationship and could discuss anything. I asked Mindy how the sex was going and she blushed and smiled with delight and told me that it was getting better all the time.

Mindy, asked about me and I told her that I have had sex with three girls this month and I thought it was more of a "NEAT" thing than anything else. I told Mindy that I thought the challenge of getting the girl to go to bed with me was the real thrill for me.

Mindy, looked at me and told me that she did not think that was a good thing as I would not have a nice relationship with anybody that way. The nice relationship was what made the sex so nice, Mindy said.

I hear you Mindy, but I don't feel anything for any of these girls, I just wanted to have sex. Maybe later when

I find that special girl I will understand what you mean, Mindy. But, for now I was just having a good time.

Yes, Mort, what about the girls, you are really just using them. Mindy, we all still young kids, they know there is no relationship there on the first or second or third dates. If they wanted to wait for a relationship then they did not have to have sex with me. It was their choice, it's not like I forced anyone to do anything.

Our conversation was interrupted as Ally and Cally came into the room with their report cards in their hands and Molly was following them. I could tell by their faces that they both were not happy so they both must have had a least one bad mark and that was all I was expecting was one bad mark each.

Both Ally and Cally must have been planning on going out as they were both dressed. Ally with nice a long sleeved silk blouse and her usual ratty looking jeans with holes in them. Ally did not seem to have any class as all.

Cally was also wearing a long sleeve silk blouse but with a tight wrap around skirt that was very short together with 3 inch high heels and white knee stockings. They were both very nice looking girls, but Cally, especially dressed that way, I found her so ever fuckable.

I held out my hand and said report cards please. Both Ally and Cally handed me their reports cards. I looked at Cally's first and she had Two "C"s, two "B's and a "D" in math. Cally started to get tears in her eyes as she knew that I was going to spank her and she knew that my spankings were no pity patter, that they really hurt.

Yet, I still got the impression that Cally was more embarrassed then afraid of the spanking. Feeling Cally embarrassment made me hard again and gave me a real feeling of satisfaction.

I looked at Ally's report card and was shocked as she got Two C's and three D's. Wow! Ally, this is really a bad report card! I guess you did not take me seriously when I told you that you would get a spanking for every mark below a "C", did you?

Ally just looked at me with that nasty face of resistance, as if I could not push her around. I liked that challenge however, so it was fine with me as I would enjoy punishing her all the more. I was looking forward to making Ally scream and cry. Boy, I really wanted to hurt Ally and make her fell my authority.

However, I was so surprised by Ally's report card I told her to go and stand in the corner as I wanted some more time to think about it as I could not give her three spankings. After just one spanking Ally's ass will be all black and blue for a couple of weeks so I could not spank her again for a least two to three weeks for a second time and that just did not seem all that effective to me.

Beside, suppose something else comes up and I would not be able to spank her for that either. If she ever figured that out, she would start to misbehaving even more figuring there was nothing I could do about it.

So I sent Ally went off to the corner and I got up and took my seat on the spanking chair. Mindy and Molly both stayed to watch. Ally could also see from her corner

as she could see by looking in the mirror. I also noticed that Sabrina was watching from the kitchen.

Cally, being the good girl, knew what was going to happen and did not fight me as she followed me over to the spanking chair. I almost felt sorry for Cally as she was usually very good and hardly even got into any trouble and was already starting to cry from shame and or embarrassment.

I wondered if Cally was embarrassed because she got a "D" or if it was because she was going to get a spanking and this time the Spanking was going to be in front of everyone else and was not just Cally and I like her very first spanking.

Regardless, I knew this spanking would actually benefit Cally. The first spanking that I gave Cally ended up with her keeping her room clean. As I knew that Cally was way too smart to be getting poor marks I thought that this spanking would wake her up and that she would try harder in school and get better marks in the future.

I really thought that I was doing Cally a favor by spanking her, at least that was what I was telling myself. I really did hope that was true as I had no reason to want to spank Cally like I did with Ally and Sabrina.

Cally was wearing that tight skirt so I had to roll it up a little to get to her panties. This had a down side for Cally as without the skirt covering her in the front, Cally's pussy would be exposed to my eyes when I lower her panties.

However, still, Cally showed no resistance as I started to

lower her panties. Cally's pussy was now right there in my face. Yet Cally did not try to move away or to cover herself, rather, Cally just cried a little harder from her embarrassment.

I was sure that Cally did not want me looking at her pussy and I tried not to all that much as her mom, Molly, was sitting right there watching me.

However, after I pushed Cally's panties down to her knees I could not help it and did take a peek at her pussy as I raised up my head and then pointed to my lap with the brush and Cally took her place over my lap.

I probably did not spank Cally as hard or as long as maybe I should have spanked her, but she was crying all out after only 10 spanks and I thought that giving her the same long hard spanking I love to give to her sister Ally was not necessary for Cally.

I also again realized that I did not enjoy spanking Cally as much as Ally or Sabrina as they had this rebellious attitude about them and Cally was just very submissive and accepting of my authority.

After all, Cally allowed me to lower her panties, look at her pussy, and climbed over my lap without having any reaction that would signal anything but obedience and acceptance of my authority in this house. I had to really respect Cally for that, as I know it must be have been so hard for her to control herself in that manner.

Nevertheless, I did enjoy watching Cally's ass turn all sorts of red and darker red and then some black and blue. I loved watching Cally wiggle her fine plump ass

all over my lap and vibrate my rock hard cock at the same time.

I enjoyed listening to Cally cry and cry and cry some more. I also knew that Cally could feel my rock hard cock against her hip as she wiggled around and that did not seem to bother her as she did not try to move an another way to avoid that contact.

But, with Cally, the crying came easily as she did not fight it at all. Cally seemed to act like she knew that she earned the spanking and deserved the spanking. Unlike Ally or Sabrina who just thought I was a young rich punk who was pushing them around to be mean.

I also thought again, that with Cally the crying was much more of an emotional thing and not so much a painful thing. I guessed the embarrassment of have her panties lowered and getting a spanking from a younger smaller kid was emotionally the problem for Cally.

But, as I found out later, I was wrong. It turned out that Cally took the spanking with such bravery and composure as she did know that she deserved the spanking because she did not follow the rules. The rules about the grades.

Cally assumed as I did that the spanking would not only punish her for failing to do well, but would also encourage her to do better. Apparently up until this time in her live, there was no encouragement and that made Cally lazy.

I only gave Cally about 100 spanks and then told her that she could get up and go and stand in the corner. Cally,

as I said, was very obedient and got of my lap and again this time did not even bother to look for her panties that flew across the room as she kicked those nice legs of hers very early in the spanking.

Instead, Cally looked at me, as she did not try to cover her pussy, and told me she was sorry that she did poorly in school and she would try harder in the future. I just shook my head in affirmation as I really did not know what to say as I was not expecting such an apology from Cally. However, I sure was impressed to be getting an apology.

Cally turned around and headed for the stairs to go up and stand in the corner. Cally did not even bother to try and push her skirt down to cover her pussy as she knew that I required her to keep her ass exposed while standing in the corner after a spanking and with that tight skirt Cally could not cover the front without covering the back.

With Cally now standing in the corner next to Ally I was going to call Ally down, but I was still not sure what to do with her as her report card was far worst then Molly or me expected and therefore Ally deserved much more than a spanking. So I called Sabrina in from the kitchen and told her to get a pair of wrist cuffs and the strap, yes Sir, curtsey.

While we were waiting, Molly told Mindy that I seem to be doing a nice job training Sabrina as she seems so much more cooperative and obedient now and she even does a better job of cleaning the house.

Molly even noted that she always wondered why our

mom kept Sabrina around as she was not a very good maid. Mindy's responded in agreement with both of those points, but noted again, that she thought I may be going too far with my methods.

Sabrina came back with the strap and the wrist cuffs. I called Ally to come back down to the living room and I told Sabrina to put the wrist cuffs on her and hook them tight behind Ally's back, yes Sir, curtsey.

My cock was still hard from enjoying that spanking I just gave to Cally so it was certainly not going down anytime soon. Since Ally was wearing pants, I told Sabrina to remove them, which left Ally standing there in her panties.

I took Ally by the shoulders and moved her over in front of one of the couch arms and pushed her over so the her hips were on top of the couch arm and her face was deep into the cushion, leaving her legs to hang over the side of the couch.

The net effect was that I was going to have one great looking ass sticking straight up at me so that I could give it a good beating with that big thick strap.

I lowered Ally's panties down to her ankles. I knew that the panties would soon be flying across the room anyway, but I still did not remove them myself. I guessed I like Ally to kick them off.

With Ally in that position her ass looked simply fantastic and I also got a nice long look at her pussy lips. This was not the view I got when Ally was over my knees getting a spanking as from that position I really could not see

their pussies. I thought that Ally had a real nice pussy and I liked looking at it and I wondered if Cally would be just as nice as they were twins.

Nevertheless, I picked up the strap as I had a job to do and that job was not looking at pussies. I lifted the strap up over my head and WHACK! WHACK! WHACK! WHACK! WHACK! The strap sounded like a shotgun going off considering the echo in the living room. There were 5 welts developing before my eyes. Those developing welts on that great looking ass was some of the best eye candy I had ever seen.

WHACK! WHACK! WHACK! WHACK! WHACK! Ally was screaming her head off with each WHACH! and she was already crying freely. The 10 WHACKS so far covered all of her ass cheeks from the top to the bottom. There was also 10 real nice welts on the right side of Ally's cheek from where the straps tail wrapped around to the side of her right cheek.

WHACK! WHACK! WHACK! WHACK! WHACK! WHACK! That was fifteen from the one side and Ally was struggling the best she could to get off the couch, but in that position with her hands cuffed behind her back she was not going anywhere.

I gave Ally one lick every 10 seconds so after 25 licks four minutes of nothing but pain for Ally. I was hitting her about a hard as I could. I wanted to punish Ally, I wanted to hurt Ally, I wanted Ally to take all that pain and I wanted Ally to learn to obey me. I was loving all this power and I was loving listening to Ally scream and cry thereby verifying how much she was in pain.

I change sides and WHACK! WHACK! WHACK! WHCAK! WHACK! I started to lick Ally's ass from the other side so I could cover her left side of her left cheek with those same nice bright welts that are still growing on her right side. The sides of Ally's ass were showing the growing welts so much better the center of the cheeks as there is little or no padding on the sides.

WHACK! WHACK! WHACK! WHACK! WHACK! Molly looked at me as if to say that she thought that Ally had enough as Ally sounded like she could not scream or cry anymore as she was losing her energy level to be able to kick her legs with the same veracity. I smiled to Molly and just shook my head that I understood.

WHACK! WHACK! WHACK! WHACK! WHACK! That was 25 from that side and I was finished. This was the first time that I had strapped Ally and judging by her reaction I would bet she was getting the message and when I tell her that she better get at least all "C"s, I will bet next time she will, but we will see.

I laid the strap down and took a seat and just watched Ally lay there crying her head off and the tears were just not stopping, but hell, all the better for my enjoyment as Ally was letting me know that I really did a good job of strapping her, of punishing her, of hurting her, this was great I thought.

I asked Molly if she was going to stay for a while and she said no that she had somewhere to go. So I told Sabrina to get ice teas for Mindy and me, yes Sir, curtsey.

By the time Sabrina came back with the ice tea, Ally seemed to have calmed down enough to send her back

to the corner so I told Sabrina to help her up, tuck her skirt into her cuffs so she could go back to stand in the corner with my handiwork on full display, yes Sir, curtsey.

Sabrina did as she was told. I looked at Mindy and said, see how obedient Sabrina is getting and her house work has improved also. Mindy, looked at me and said, I do see, but be careful bother.

I was not sure what I needed to be careful of, after all, I was the Boss around here, if they did not like it then they could leave, I was not stopping them.

Sabrina, yes Sir? Walk Ally up the stairs to the corner as she may be unsteady on her feet. Yes Sir, curtsey. Also, Sabrina, when you get up there bring Cally back down with you, yes Sir, curtsey.

Sabrina walked Ally up the stairs and put her back in the corner and told Cally to come with her and Cally started to go back down the stairs when Sabrina stopped her and pushed he skirt back down so her pussy was still not out in the open.

Sabrina brought Cally back to stand in front of me and I asked Cally if she learned her lesson? Yes Sir, Cally said, with a tear still in her eye. So no more bad marks Cally? No Sir, not one, not ever! Good Cally, then you are dismissed.

Thank you sir, Cally said. I really enjoyed Cally's attitude and maybe more so, her statement in fact that she would never get another bad mark. That was quite a confident statement and I hoped Cally would make it true. I did

not mind if I never got to punish Cally again, it was Ally and Sabrina that I enjoyed punishing.

As you know, this was the second time I needed to spank Cally in just over two months, but still Cally is the good girl of the house. Cally tries to be a good kid and obeys me in every way and always speaks to me with respect. Cally seems to appreciate the fact that she has a great house to live in and has a great life here and she acts like it.

Additionally, unlike Sabrina and Ally, Cally did not seem to blame me for spanking her. Cally did not seem to think that I was just mean for spanking her like the other two did. Cally seemed to understand that she was being spanked because she deserved the spanking in accordance with the house rules and since she broke the rules, she earned the spanking.

I thought Cally's attitude was the much better attitude. Maybe it was Cally's better attitude that made her the better behaved person that she was. Cally just seemed so bright and so special to me, so different then Ally.

Mindy and I continued to chat about other things while we continued to look thru the mail. Mindy asked me if I did not think that I was too tough on Ally as I was much easier on Cally. I told Mindy that Ally needs much harsher treatment as she is so rebellious and has a nasty attitude and that was reflected in her marks. So, no, I told Mindy, that Ally needs to be punished much more harshly.

After Mindy and I were though with the mail and finished our chat, I called Ally back down to the living

room. Ally came down with her hands still bond behind her and stood in front of me.

Now, as Ally stood in front of me this time, without the benefit of a dress or skirt to drop down and cover her pussy, I got a real nice look at Ally's pussy from the front, as Ally had no panties or pants to cover her. Boy, my cock enjoyed that!

Ally, as further punishment for that report card, you are to come directly home from school every day for the next two weeks and do your homework. Then you are to stand in the corner with your hands bond behind you back as you are now and your skirt raised and your panties lowered to your knees for 30 minutes each day, for 14 days. Understand Ally? Yes Sir. Boy, if looks could kill?

Things were pretty quiet for the next two weeks both at home and in school. Sabrina continued to be relatively obedient and her housework was better as well. I loved all the French maid uniforms that Sabrina had to wear now and I loved to see her curtsey to me all the time.

One day Sabrina missed a curtsey and I made her stand in the corner for 30 minutes. She never forgot to curtsey to me again.

I had sex with two more girls, it was all just fun for me. I never cared about them and once I fucked them I never took them out again. Meanwhile, I was enjoying the hell out of having Sabrina drop to her knees and give me a blow job whenever I told her too. I could tell that Sabrina did not want too, but I think that made it even better for me.

However, I did find some time to label another three kids. I wondered why there always seemed that there were three of everyone, but hell, that's just the way it was.

Anyway, I now had a new name for a group of kids, "The three Fags" They always hung around together and I always wondered how bad it must be to be a faggot. After all, they sucked each other's cocks and fucked each other in the ass. How sick was that???????

I could not imagine how bad it would be for a guy to take a cock in his ass. I mean, ass fucking is for girls, not men. I knew they did stuff like that in prison, but because they liked it? It gave me shivers. The same for having another guys cock in your mouth, I could throw up just thinking about it.

Anyway, like the other labels, the three fags stuck and there was a few more guys who hated me.

SABRINA GETS THE STRAP AND GETS IT IN THE ASS:

It was two days before Thanksgiving and I continued to struggle with Sabrina and her attitude. I was making some progress as at least when I told her to do something she obeyed me. Sabrina was becoming a better maid as she was cleaning better and keeping up with my schedule of requirements.

Sabrina was even getting better at giving me my blow jobs whenever I wanted one, which was usually twice maybe three times a week. I really like standing up and looking down and see Sabrina on her knees with my cock in her mouth.

Although, I wondered if I liked that position so much because it was the only time Sabrina was shorter than me. After all, in those five inch high heels I make her wear, she is about 10 inches taller than me.

However, in spite of all the improvements with Sabrina, her attitude about smiling and saying yes Sir and more importantly not making faces of hate at me was still a problem. For example, the other day when I wanted a blow job, Sabrina just dropped to her knees in front of me

and did not say yes sir, did not curtsey, and made a mean face at me, like she thought that I was disgusting.

Sure the blow job was nice and I enjoyed it, but I expect her to be able to give me a blow job, with the yes Sir, with the curtsey, and with a smile. I mean, is that too much to ask, I did not think so! Additionally, Sabrina has never learned to give me blow jobs as depicted in the written information I gave her.

One day I told Sabrina that I wanted her to clean the kitchen more often than once per day. I told her that I wanted it cleaned well once each day, but that she should also clean up after each use as I did not like to walk into a messy kitchen. Sabrina, instead of giving me a smile and a yes Sir, I just got one of her faces that showed her disgust with me.

I had verbally noted to Sabrina several times that I did not find that acceptable, but apparently Sabrina only understands punishment and not words. It seemed that the nicer and more forgiving I tried to be with Sabrina, the more she regressed.

I looked at Sabrina and her disrespecting face and just told her to go and stand in the corner. Sabrina, looked at me again with contempt in her eyes, but at least she huffed herself off to the corner.

I went to my room and got out the big thick strap as I thought that I would give that a try as so far Sabrina had been spanked and whipped but has not been strapped. I was looking forward to using the strap, so that night was as good as any night, I thought. I was also planning

to fuck Sabrina in the ass after the strapping. We'll see if she likes that?

I don't know if Sabrina has had anal sex before, but I have not and it looked like fun from what I saw on the internet. When I was looking up maid information I found a lot of information on what were called "sissy maids". They were male French maid whores. It seemed that one of the training methods they used on the sissy maids was to fuck them in the ass.

It was suppose to hurt if the "fucker" was not gentle about it and just shoved his cock up the maids ass. I guess that does not allow any time for the maid to get use to having a cock invade their ass. I understand that prisoners also use this method to hurt other prisoners.

So I was willing to give it a try to see if it would help train that bitch, Sabrina. The anal theory as I read on the internet was that it made one feel very submissive getting fucked in the ass. While I thought that may be especially true for sissy maid men getting fucked in the ass, I was not sure the same would be true for a women who may do that voluntary anyway.

I knew that I was going to have to tie her up real tight, not only to take the strapping that I was going to give her, as I had full intention to have her howling and crying and screaming before I was finished laying that strap to Sabrina's bare ass.

Sabrina just does not seem to get the fact that I am her boss now and that she will obey me and act the way I want her too or that I will have the greatest time beating her. So I could not really lose either way, I will either get

the respectful and submissive service I wanted or I get to beat her, a win, win for me, I thought, and so did my cock, which was rock hard just thinking about that strap and Sabrina's ass.

I put everything I needed on my bed and went down to get Sabrina. At least she was standing in the corner correctly with her hands cuffed behind her back with the wrist cuffs. I unhooked the cuffs from behind her back and re cuffed them in front of her and told her to follow me and again she did not say yes Sir.

When we got back to my room I told her to lay over the side of the bed with her hips on the side so her legs were over the side of the bed. I hooked a long thin leather strap to her wrist cuffs and hooked the other end to a hook I installed under the bed frame and used the buckle on the one end of the leather strap and pulled it taunt.

I went around to the other side of the bed and told her to lift up her hips while I put a big pillow under her hips to lift her ass up in the air to give me a better target. Then I put two ankle cuffs on her ankles and with another long thin leather strap I attached her ankles to a wall hook that I installed and pulled her legs taught.

I went back around to the front of Sabrina and pulled the leather strap holding the wrist cuffs a bit tighter as I wanted to make sure that she was not going anywhere as my strapping was really going to hurt her.

I also figured that when I fucked her in the ass that she was really going to screaming. That was fine with me, I

wanted to hear Sabrina scream and scream and scream and cry and cry some more.

From what I had read, the ass fucking will hurt her even more then the strapping. But, I understand that the secret was to use plenty of lubricant so when I forced my cock thru Sabrina's ass hole it would not tear her anus and cause her to bleed. I did not want to damage Sabrina, I just want to hurt Sabrina and make her more obedient and more submissive to me.

Sabrina was pretty cooperative thru this punishment so far. She stood in the corner properly and did not say a word as I walked her down to my room and tied her up real tight. I guess she was at least learning the she only had two choices, go home or obey me. So far, she has chosen obedience but with a bad attitude.

I read some information on the internet about training submissives and the main theory was that the dominate needs to punish the subject often enough and severely enough to break their attitude so that the subject can overcome their own internal feeling of resistance so they get to the point where they understand cooperation is in their best interest and in many cases actually enjoy the submission, even if it is temporally until the situation changes.

One of the examples I read about would be the prison environment where men who have no homosexual tendencies learn to enjoy having sex either with other men from the dominate or from the submissive side.

The prisoners seem to accept this new way of life as it become their reality and fighting it does not produce

any good results. Accepting this allows them to be safer and more comfortable under the circumstances. However, when they leave prison, they go back to being the same heterosexuals they were prior to prison life and no longer have a desire to anal sex or oral sex with other men.

So I thought that the way to continue to train Sabrina was to praise her for the things that she did well or was very cooperative with and continue to punished her as often as possible for the areas that she continues to resist.

So, as I noted before, the housework itself is where Sabrina has made the most improvement and her poor attitude towards me is what she needs to have beaten out of her and I was happy to do it.

I went around to the front of Sabrina and told her to look at me. As Sabrina did, I began to scold her, telling her that she knows by now what I expect for her. Two, with my money I could always hire another maid that would be happy to do all the things that I expect from her.

Three, the only reason I don't fire her and get another maid is because I enjoy punishing her so much and the new maid would not need to be punished, at least not very often.

So, BITCH, if you decide to stay here after tonight and you still want to be my maid and you chose not to go home you need to know that I love punishing you. I love making you get on your knees and suck my cock. I love making you curtsey and say yes Sir all the time to me.

So, unless you want to be punished all the time, I suggest that you obey me with the proper attitude in the future. Otherwise, there is a lot more hairbrush, strap, cane, and or whippings in your future. Sabrina did not say anything, she just dropped her head into the bed.

I picked up the strap and thought that I would scare Sabrina a bit before I started. I grabbed the back of Sabrina's head with her hair and picked her head up so she had to look at me.

I showed Sabrina the strap, it was over three feet long, about an inch and a half wide and was very thick. I had Sabrina look at it and told her that maybe this strap will help with your attitude. She just looked at me with those challenging eyes and I dropped her head by letting go of her hair.

I walked back around to the other side and flipped up Sabrina's ever so short French maid dress and pulled down her panties and raised the strap up over my head and WHACK! I hit her across the ass as hard as I could and all she did was moan a bit. However, what I saw I liked as a big welt started developing before my eyes across Sabrina's beautiful ass cheeks.

I just stood there and waited for about 20 or 30 seconds watching the welt get darker and darker. I love how the welt looked across Sabrina's nice firm ass. WHACK! and another welt started to grow and WHACK! and another welt. WOW! This was really fun and WHACK! as now Sabrina has four growing welts and the last one actually got a sound of unhappiness out of Sabrina mouth.

Sabrina was making me think that I was not hurting her.

I thought that that would not serve her well because I was not about to stop until I thought that she was well punished and that will not be until she was in tears and crying her head off.

WHACK! WHACK! WHACK! and this time I made sure that the strap not only hit across her ass cheeks, but it also wrapped over and around the right cheek so the tail end of the strap would provide the welt coverage to the side of her ass cheek as well. I did that with Ally and she screamed her head off.

This additional coverage got a much better ouch and moan from Sabrina so I thought I was making progress. WHACK! WHACK! WHACK! WHACK! WHACK! Now Sabrina was starting to scream a little after each WHACK! and WHACK! and Sabrina started to cry. Now I was having real fun as WHACK! WHACK! WHACK! I was getting a nice scream and some real tears.

I loved watching the welts grow and grow and turn a dark color and WHACK! WHACK! That was a nice scream there with that WHACK! and the tears are flowing nicely now, so much for her pretending that I was not hurting her.

I moved over the Sabrina's other side so I could get all those nice welts on both sides of her ass cheeks. The right side was well welted as there was no un welted skin left. WHACK! WHACK! WHACK! WHACK! WHACK! The other side was starting to fill in nicely with welts also, but more importantly, Sabrina was screaming quite loudly now and she was crying in earnest so I knew I was having more fun now.

WHACK! WHACK! WHACK! WHACK! WHACK! Now I was having even more fun as Sabrina was crying uncontrollably and struggling against her bonds and wiggling all over the place as she screamed after each WHACK! WHACK! WHACK! WHACK! WHACK!

There I thought that was about 40 whacks and Sabrina had no resistance left whatsoever in her now, she was crying so hard I almost felt sorry for her, but I smiled and thought to myself that I did a good job of strapping that disrespectful bitch.

I put the strap back on the bed and got undressed. I walked back around to the front of Sabrina and again picked up her head by pulling the back of her head up by grabbing her hair and not in a gentle way. Sabrina's makeup was a mess as the tears caused it to be dripping down her face and smeared it all over her cheeks.

Sabrina, obviously from her shame, for being strapped by this young punk, as she viewed me, still looked down even though I was holding her head up. I told her to look at me and she moved her eyes upward to look at me and I did not see any hate this time in those eyes, just the eyes of a well punished Sabrina.

I knew that Sabrina noticed that I was sporting a nice hard erection, but she had no idea that I intended to use it on her yet. Sabrina showed no emotion except to continue to cry and whimper.

I looked at Sabrina, already being very pleased with myself and very well entertained by her punishment so far. So, I decided to tell Sabrina that I was now going got

fuck her in the ass! I just wanted to see her reaction, I thought that it may be a lot of fun.

It was a good thing I tired her up every tight as she started to struggle like she never struggled before and started to scream and say NO! NO! NO! NO! NO! DON'T! NO! DON'T! I will obey for sir, Please sir, I will obey you sir.

I guess I now had Sabrina's attention. But her screaming was music to my ears and I thought she would be screaming even more when my cock was in her ass. I told Sabrina that she does not give the orders around here, I do, and as soon as she learns that the better off she will be and I dropped her head and she started to cry even harder. Sabrina struggled again her bonds even harder, but she was going nowhere.

I walked back around to Sabrina's ass side and squeezed some of this lube stuff I bought from the tube and smeared it all over my cock so it would slid in Sabrina's ass without too much friction. Remember my goal was to make her ass fucking hurt as much as I could, by stretching the anus muscles. But I did not want to rip her open where she needed time to heal or need stitches to close her up.

Sabrina was still shaking her head no, and trying to say NO! thru her tears and thru her crying and thru her struggling but she was getting the point that it was doing no good and she calmed down some.

I stepped up between Sabina's legs and used my hands to spread her ass cheeks and put my cock right up against her ass hole and pressed a little forward. Sabrina

screamed and tried to wiggle her ass away from me, but I had her secured well enough.

I waited until Sabrina calmed a bit and started to push my cock into her ass hole. Sabrina bucked and wiggled and bucked some more as she screamed again and cried even harder. However, I did not think Sabrina was helping herself as the more she wiggled the more she sort of wiggled my cock into her ass hole not out of her ass hole.

Just after Sabrina realized that my cock was all the way inside her, she started yelling, please stop, please stop, I will be good, I will be good, I will obey you, I will obey you. Please Sir, Sabrina tried to say the best as she could while still crying very hard.

I did not stop, but I did hold still with my cock still inside her ass as I thought for a few seconds. I thought that maybe I should stop as I was feeling a bit sorry for Sabrina as that was the first time Sabrina ever begged me to stop. Sabrina took her whipping without begging me to stop.

Sabrina took her strapping without begging me to stop. So I guess there was something to what I read on the internet about fucking in the ass, even though she was a women. Yet, I still did not know if she was begging me to stop because I was hurting her or because she just did not want me to fuck her in the ass.

Regardless, I told Sabrina that she should have thought about that before she disrespected me. With that I pushed my cock into her ass hole even harder and she

bucked like a wide horse, but that just forced my cock to go in further without my help.

I just tried to keep my position as Sabrina bucked and cried and screamed a little more. Sabrina, thru her tears and stuffy nose and her crying like a little girl tried to beg me off again by repeating that I win that she will obey me from now on and she will respect me and my authority, please "BOSS" Sabrina called me for the first time ever. Please Sir, please have mercy on me, please Sir!

I told Sabrina that she choose to learn the hard way. This was happening because you disobeyed me and this is happening because you disrespected me. Now, Sabrina it is too late to beg. Now, Sabrina you need to take the punishment that you have she earned. Now, Sabrina, you need to take the punishment you brought upon yourself. I was showing Sabrina that I would never back down from any punishment.

At that I started to fuck her and slid my cock in and out of her ass hole. The whole time that I was fucking her and she was bucking and bucking the better it felt for me, not only physically better, but emotionally better as I was enjoying the hell out of Sabrina's suffering.

I wanted to punish Sabrina with that strap and I strapped her real good. I wanted to hurt Sabrina by fucking her in the ass and now I was hurting her by fucking her in the ass real good.

I wanted this ass fucking to hurt Sabrina and hurt the whole time and hurt as much as I could make it hurt, Sabrina was being punished and I wanted to make sure

she knew that I was punishing her. The Boss of this house!

After a minute or so of slow fucking Sabrina seemed to be getting use to having my cock in her ass so I started to speed up the action while I was still enjoying the great look of all those welts on her ass as her ass cheeks were all black and blue and I could see all the overlapping strap marks.

Then I was fucking Sabrina in the ass as hard as I could with my balls slapping against her pussy with each and every hard thrust. Sabrina continued to cry and now she was grunting as I slammed my cock in her ass each time.

I was not sure, but thought that Sabrina was starting to enjoy it, but at this point I did not care as I was having a great time and then I exploded inside Sabrina with one of the best orgasms of my young life. That was great I thought, I will be fucking Sabrina in the ass a lot in the future I said to myself.

I pulled my cock out of Sabrina's ass and went into the bathroom and cleaned my cock off. When I got back Sabrina was still crying, but very lightly. I unhooked Sabrina's legs and she just laid there. I went around and unhooked Sabrina's wrists as well and she just laid there.

I was guessing that I had beaten and fucked the fight out of her. I was going to get a towel and clean her ass of the mess I made smearing my cum all over her ass as I fucked her. But, I thought that I should not show any kindness and decided against it.

Instead I went around to the other side of the bed and told her to get up! Yes Sir, Sabrina said thru her tears, so maybe we are getting somewhere I thought. I helped her get off the bed and found that she was a little shaky on her feet.

After Sabrina steadied herself, I hooked her hands behind her back again and told her to return to the corner. I knew that while she was standing in the corner showing off her brightly welted ass to everyone else in the house, that my cum would be leaking down the inside of her legs and that would most likely be very shameful and humiliating for Sabrina. Just thinking about her humiliation gave me an erection again.

I went down to the kitchen and got a snack and found Mindy there having dinner. I said hello and she said that she saw Sabrina's ass and asked me what I used and I told her about the strap that I bought.

Mindy said that I must have beat Sabrina really hard based on all the noise she was making and the condition of her ass. I told Mindy that Sabrina was just not getting the idea as to who's boss around here.

So what's that stuff dripping down the inside of her legs Mindy asked? Cum, I said. Mort, you had sex with her too, Mindy asked?. Well, not really, I took her in the ass. Oh my! Mindy said, that explains the extra screaming.

I asked Mindy if she ever tried that and she told me that she did once, but it hurt so much that she stopped Jim and has not tried it again. So, you must have really hurt Sabrina, HUH? She asked. I wanted to hurt her and I

think I did a good job of it, Mindy, I wanted to punish that bitch.

Mindy did not have anything further to say and we chatted about other things while we ate together. Mindy did tell me that she did not think that any good boy would be taking Sabrina in the ass, only bad boys do such things, you think about that brother. I thought about it for a few seconds and then forgot to think about it anymore.

As we were leaving the kitchen, Mindy again told me that she understood the strap and the whip and the hairbrush, but taking Sabrina in the ass, don't you think you are going too far, Mort?

I looked at Mindy and told her that Sabrina could go back to South America at any time if she did not like it here, yet she chooses to stay. Yea, I know, Mindy said, but that part does not sit well with me, that's all I'm saying, Mort.

I went to see Sabrina and she was still there standing in the corner and indeed she had plenty of my cum dripping down the inside of her legs. Sabrina's ass being uncovered as I require was looking great not only because Sabrina had a nice ass, but all the welts I found to be most attractive.

I did not bother to ask Sabrina if she was ready to obey me this time as I already went thru that after the whipping I gave her and she must have forgot, so I figured we would see, hell, I can always beat her some more, I thought.

I unhooked Sabrina's wrist cuffs and told her that her

punishment was over and she could go and get cleaned up and get back to work. Sabrina, turned around and dropped her skirt down and gave me a nice curtsey and a very polite yes Sir, thank you Sir.

The next morning I saw Sabrina in the hallway and she gave me a nice curtsey and a nice smile and a nice good morning Sir. Good morning I also said to Sabrina. I guess we will see how long that lasts?

THANKSGIVING:

One of the times that Mindy and I use to really enjoy as a family was Thanksgiving dinner. Our mom use to make the dinner. Then mom and Sabrina and Mindy would all help serving and or making some of the meal. However, at Thanksgiving, Sabrina was part of the family and got to eat with everyone else.

I spoke with Mindy about this for this year, our first year without our parents. Mindy thought that we should continue that pattern. So, we spoke with Molly and we all agreed that the ladies would all share making and serving Thanksgiving dinner and Sabrina could be part of the family for the day.

I had a small problem with Sabrina being part of the family at any time, but I agreed to keep Mindy happy. Molly ended up being the cook and she did a great job. Ally did almost nothing, Sabrina set the table and took care of all of the drinks. Mindy and Cally helped making pies and Molly became the director for the day.

At dinner time Mindy, Molly, Cally, and Sabrina all wore nice dresses. Ally showed up in a pair of torn jeans and a rock concert T shirt. I found that to be unacceptable and told Ally that she needed to dress like a lady for once in her life as she always dressed like a slob.

Cally never wore clothes that were torn or dirty or sloppy. Even though Molly had little money, Cally at least look presentable and clean. While Ally always looked like she came from and an "ally". The only time Ally looked nice was in her school uniform.

Anyway, all I got from Ally was a nasty face and then she asked, OH!, I suppose you are going to tell me how to dress now. I looked at Ally and told her that as long as she lives here I will tell her whatever I want. NOW!, It's Thanksgiving and I don't want to spoil the day for everyone by giving you the spanking that you are asking for, Ally!

However, Ally! It's a nice dress or a spanking, you chose! Ally chose the dress and went and changed and came back looking better than I had ever seen her look. Even Molly, said, WOW! Ally, you look like a real lady!

We all seemed to have a very nice dinner. Molly turned out to be a very good cook. Ally, spent the day making faces and being unset with the world. Mindy and Sabrina and Molly chatted about all kinds of stuff.

But, the thing that surprised me was Cally. Cally did not say all that much as she did not really take part in all the simple gossip and chit chat of the other three females. Instead, Cally, spoke to me the most and we discussed all kinds of things about math and science and finance.

These were subjects that I enjoyed but no longer had anyone who could entertain an intelligent discussion with since my father died. During our discussion I discovered that Cally could play chess. I did beat her

later that day in three straight games, but she was not a bad player.

I guess I can judge such things as I was the best chess player around these parts. Within a year of my father teaching me to play chess when I was 12, I could beat him almost every time. I could beat the best players in the chess club at school and I could even beat the chess club teacher.

However, my focus this day was on how smart Cally seemed to be. In my opinion Cally seemed so much smarter than the marks she got in school.

Nevertheless, Cally was the highlight of the day for me as I really enjoyed speaking with her about all these subjects and she gave me a slight challenge with the chess games.

I did not see any of these traits in Ally, she sounded dumb and acted dumb and dressed like someone with no class.

Overall, the day was a big success and everyone seemed to have a real nice time. Molly, Sabrina, Cally, and Mindy all help clean up, but not Ally.

NO! Of course, I did not help, I was a guy and the Boss of the house, all those girls were here to serve me!

Sabrina and the Cane:

It was the second week in December and Sabrina was behaving rather well since I gave her that strapping and fucked her in the ass. Sabrina was even friendly to everyone over Thanksgiving dinner. Sabrina was not even making faces at me when I would make her get down in her knees and suck my cock a couple of times a week.

Come to think of it, Ally has been really good as well, I have not had to punish her since the last report card in the beginning of November, over a month ago. I didn't know how she is doing in school, but at least she was keeping her room clean and was polite to everyone.

Anyway, back to Sabrina, I started to notice that her cleaning was getting more sloppy and the house looked more dirty. I was not sure exactly what was going on, but the house just did not look as clean as Sabrina was keeping it.

After dinner one night I started to tell Sabrina what I thought. Sabrina just looked at me with that nasty face that I use to see and told me that I was nothing but a spoiled rich punk. Nothing makes you happy, you son of a bitch.

Well, that was not good. How dare Sabrina call my mother a bitch? Yes, I know that Sabrina did not mean to disrespect my mother, but her attitude and what came out of her mouth was still unacceptable.

I just sat there shocked at Sabrina's outburst. Sabrina realized what she had said and dropped to her knees in front of me and kept telling me over and over again how sorry she was.

I looked at Sabrina and just told her to go and stand in the corner. Sabrina, knew better than to say anything other than yes Sir, stand up and curtsey and go and stand in the corner. I just could not believe Sabrina's mouth.

All Sabrina needed to do was listen to me and say she would try to do better and that would have been the end of it, unless things did not improve. But, the mouth, what was all that about?

I went to my room and went thru the days mail while Sabrina spent her time in the corner. About 20 minutes later I got the cane out of the closet and walked down the hallway to where Sabrina was standing in the corner and I told her to turn around.

I showed Sabrina the cane and told her from what I read on the internet this cane will hurt more than the strap did, but only you will know for sure Sabrina, so you will have to let me know, as I smiled like I was laughing at her.

Sabrina looked at me without her usual defiant look and

instead with fear in her eyes she said, Please Sir, please let me obey you and don't beat me, please Sir?

I just ignored what Sabrina said, but I did enjoy listening to her beg me. Follow me to the basement Sabrina, yes Sir, curtsey. I have another surprise for you Sabrina, as I turned and walked towards the basement with the cane in my hand.

When we arrived in the basement I showed Sabina a new bench that I had made based on samples I found on the internet in some of those bondage and discipline sites. It was a very sturdy wood bench with a thick leather covered top.

It was like a work bench shape or road horse shape where Sabrina would lay her body, tummy down on the long top part which was about 3 feet long and 1 foot wide with thick padding so one could lay on it comfortably for a long while.

I told Sabrina to lay across the bench and she looked at me like she was going to beg me again and then said, please Sir, please forgive me and let me obey you now? I told Sabrina that I told her before that I never forget and I never forgive, so get on the bench, yes Sir, curtsey.

Sabrina must have been scared as she already had tears forming in her eyes, which I felt was quite a submissive act from Sabrina compared to her usual hate face. I really wanted to tell her to shut up and not to beg me as it was making me feel sorry for her, but the truth was that I enjoyed listening to her beg, so I just needed to stay strong and enjoy her begging and then enjoy beating her as well.

Sabrina laid down on the top of the bench and I used a clip to bind her right wrist cuff to the front bench leg and then clip her left wrist cuff as well. Her arms were now held down but out in front of her a bit. I moved over to the back of the bench and flipped up Sabrina's dress over her waist and then pulled her panties down to her knees.

I then hooked her ankle cuffs to the back legs of the bench so that her legs were pointing downward and backward. This position left her ass slightly rounded but sticking out to provide a nice target for my cane.

Also, in this position, Sabrina's ass is in just the right position for me to fuck her in the ass or to go around to her face and stick my cock in her mouth. The legs of the bench could easily be adjusted for height to adjust for the height of different people.

I swished the cane in the air a few times and the SWISH! The cane landed across both ass cheeks and wrapped around her left ass cheek and finished on the side of her ass where there is no plumpness to protect her. WOW! I thought that was leaving a nice long thin welt that was growing before my eyes.

Unlike when I strapped Sabrina, she was not trying to be brave this time and she wiggled her ass real nice for me and moaned loudly and for a long time as it seemed that as the cane mark was developing the pain was getting worse.

What I had read on the internet, when the cane strikes the skin it stings a lot. However, then the pain sinks into the muscle and hurts for a longer time and even hurts

more. So the theory was to cane slowly but very hard to allow the pain from each stroke to grow before adding another stroke.

That way, each stroke adds more and more pain, sort of like building a fire by putting more logs in it. This was supposed to be different from the strap which hurt a lot on contact but has no accumulating effect.

Also, with the strap, Sabrina's ass became swollen and lessened the pain as the strapping went along. With the cane, that is not suppose to happen, so I could cane Sabrina even longer.

SWISH! And I got another big struggle from Sabrina, I loved how she wiggled her ass when I was strapping her and now I get the same thrill with the cane. SWISH! And Sabrina has three nice welts growing before my eyes. I gave her four more SWISHES! Over the next minute and Sabrina started to cry and scream a little.

I was getting this effect with just 6 SWISHES!, That was much better then with the strap. I was wondering, SWISH! if Sabrina was crying sooner because she, SWISH! of her more submissive attitude, in other words, did she stop fighting me or trying to show me that I was not hurting her. Or, SWISH! Was the cane just hurting her more than the strap?

SWISH! SWISH! SWISH! SWISH! SWISH! Now I have Sabrina's attention as she is in real pain. Sabrina did not seem to have any fight left in her as already she was freely crying her heart out and screaming with each SWISH! After this first dozen I stopped and walked

around to Sabrina's face and asked her if she is ready to obey me?

Sabrina looked up at me and with the tears smearing her makeup all down her face chocked out a very quiet yes Sir, Please Sir let me obey you. Then Sabrina cried even harder, much to my delight, as I knew the additional tears were from her extreme humiliation and I was just loving that.

I told Sabrina that I was not ready to let her obey me yet, I am not finished punishing you. I just got a big sigh from Sabrina and I walked around to her back side again but on her right side instead of her left side and SWISH! SWISH! SWISH! SWISH! SWISH!

I was loving beating Sabrina with this cane as I was loving how all the welt marks that were developing on her ass cheeks and I was loving watching that real nice ass of Sabrina's wiggle all over in pain, and I loving listening to Sabrina scream and cry her eyes out.

SWISH! SWISH! SWISH! SWISH! SWISH! This is so much fun I was thinking as I gave Sabrina two more extra hard SWISH! and SWISH! and I just listened to Sabrina scream extra loud and listened to her enhanced crying and I was having a great time. I gave Sabrina 48 hard SWISHES! and she had 48 nice dark red and purple welts across her ass cheeks with 24 welts on each side of her ass.

I walked back around to Sabrina's face and watched her cry for a minute or so. Just watching Sabrina cry and cry and cry was a thrill all by itself I thought. I waited until she calmed down a bit and asked her if she was

ready to obey me now, yes Sir she managed to get out between the tears and gasping for air as her nose was clogged with snot.

I almost stopped caning Sabrina at this point, but then I thought about it and decided that she needed a real lesson so that she would never speak to me like that again. So I decided that I was going to make a real statement right here and now.

SWISH! SWISH! SWISH! SWISH! SWISH! SWISH! SWISH! SWISH! SWIAH! SWISH! SWISH! SWISH! I had Sabrina screaming her head off with each stroke as she chocked for air as she was crying so nice and so loud, I was loving it, I was just loving punishing Sabrina and hurting Sabrina. Life was great, but I was not finished beating her yet and I changed sides again.

SWISH! SWISH! SWISH! SWISH! SWISH! SWISH! SWISH! SWISH! SWISH! SWISH! SWISH! SWISH! I was having such a good time beating Sabrina. I loved her Sabrina's all by itself, but now with about 75 welts all over it, it just seemed to be even better looking to me. I loved listening to Sabrina cry so much that I would enjoy beating her for no other reason than to hear her suffer, to hear her cry.

I went back around to Sabrina's face again and said how about now, are you ready to obey me now I asked again as I smiled in laughter at her. Sabrina could not really talk as she was crying so loud, so I went back around to her back side and just enjoyed another look at the fine ass of her with all those nice welts.

As Sabrina slowed her crying somewhat, I went around

to her face again and said how about now Sabrina, are you ready to obey me, yes Sir, yes Sir, Sabrina chocked thru her tears this time. Alright then Sabrina, we'll see.

I unhooked Sabrina's wrist cuffs and then her ankle cuffs and helped her to her feet. I was enjoying looking at her face with the tears still dripping down her cheeks and all her black eye makeup flowing down her face with the tears and it gave me such a sense of satisfaction that I was able to punish Sabrina that well.

KISS OF SUBMISSION:

Once Sabrina was steady on her feet I asked her if she had ever heard of the "kiss of submission"? Sabrina told me no. I told her to drop to her knees, yes Sir, curtsey, as she dropped to her knees in front of me. I turned around so my back was facing her. I unbuckled my pants and dropped my pants and undershorts to my ankles.

Sabrina, I said, now take your hands and use each one to spread my ass cheeks and then use your lips to kiss my ass hole. I knew what was going thru Sabrina's mind as she certainly did not want to do this. NO! Of course not.

But, was she going to do it or get punished again and then she would have to do it anyway. I guess the good part about this was that my back was to Sabrina so she could make all the hate faces she wanted and I could not see her.

After some hesitation, I felt Sabrina put her hands on my ass cheeks and spread them a little and I felt "The Heat" from her mouth as her lips got closer to my ass. Sabrina actually did kiss my ass hole with her lips and then pulled her face away very quickly.

Sabrina, I said, do it again with more than one kiss, more

like you were making out with my ass hole. Sabrina tried it again and she did a little better. I knew this was humiliating Sabrina to no end and that was my goal. Embarrassing and or humiliating Sabrina was a big thrill for me.

Sabrina, your almost getting it right, now make me feel like you are loving what you are doing like I was your boyfriend and you were kissing my on my mouth. Sabrina, tried again and again she was doing a little better. Sabrina, this time I want you to use your tongue and French kiss my ass hole.

That hit the spot, Sabrina jumped to her feet and told me that I was nuts and she would never be kissing my ass hole with her tongue!!!!!

I just looked at Sabrina while I pulled my cell phone from my pocket and showed her that on speed dial I had the local immigration office. Should I press call? Sabrina? NO! SIR!, Please SIR! NO SIR! I will do it sir, I will kiss your ass for you real nice as she started crying again.

I guess the shame and humiliation of my requirements were just too much for Sabrina and she could no longer act so tough in front of this young punk. Nevertheless, I almost came just from my enjoyment of Sabrina's obvious humiliation of having to French kiss my ass hole.

Alright Sabrina, we will start again from the beginning. Now take your hands and use each one to spread my ass cheeks and then use your lips to kiss my ass hole. I knew what was going thru Sabrina's mind as I knew

that she still did not want to do this but I was loving her humiliation.

After some hesitation, I felt Sabrina put her hands on my ass cheeks and spread them a little and again I felt "The Heat" from her mouth again as it got closer to my ass. Sabrina again kissed my ass hole with her lips and then pulled her face away very quickly. Sabrina, I said, do it again with more than one kiss, more like you were making out with my ass hole. Sabrina tried it again and did a little better, like she did the first time.

Sabrina, your almost getting it right, now make me feel like you are loving what you are doing like I was your boyfriend and you were kissing my on the mouth. Sabrina, tried again and again she was doing a little better. Alright Sabrina, it is time for you to use your tongue and French kiss my ass hole.

This time I felt Sabrina's tongue all over my ass hole as she licked it and pressed her tongue against it and I did finally feel like she was trying to please me. My guess was that she really was trying to please me as she did not want any more of that cane.

Alright Sabrina, we are finished for the evening, stand up. Yes Sir, and Sabrina stood up and faced me. I told Sabrina that she was well aware that I was not happy with her progress with her obedience and respect to me.

Sabrina, you still seem to think that you have an opinion around here and you don't. Everything around here is what I say the way I say it, or you get punished Sabrina, period! Since you are struggling with idea I am going to

help you out so starting tomorrow we will have some additional obedience training for you.

Remember Sabrina this is very simple, I tell you what to do and you say yes Sir, you curtsey, and you do it, and you do it with a smile, and you do it well. Why you make it so complicated I am not sure.

Later that evening I had another chat with Mindy. Mindy asked me if I thought that I was going too far in my expectation of Sabrina and her obedience to me? I told Mindy that it had nothing to do with Sabrina or me as it's all about the money. What? Mindy questioned, money?

Yes money I told Mindy. Why do you think Sabrina stays here with me or us. Three reasons, One, she needs the money to send home to her family. Two, Sabrina cannot get a job that pays too much for her poor services like we do in her country, if she could get a job at all. Third, because we pay her much more then she can get anywhere else in this country, otherwise she would just go to another home and walk away from me and my expectations.

Yes, my sister, it is all about the money and Sabrina wants it. Sabrina wants it more then she wants to leave, that is the only reason she stays.

SABRINA'S INCREASED TRAINING BEGINS:

TRAINING DAY ONE:

The next morning Thursday morning, when we were leaving for school I told Sabrina that from now on when I get home from school that she is to find me and welcome me home and ask if she can serve me in any way, yes Sir, curtsey.

WOW, I thought that was the first time, out of all the times she has said yes Sir and curtseyed to me that she made it sound like she meant it. So, maybe I am making progress in training Sabrina to obey me, Maybe Sabrina can act like I want her to behave after all and of course, maybe not?

When I got home from school I was not in the door for 30 seconds and I saw Sabrina walking towards me. She curtseyed and said good afternoon Sir, is there anything I can do for you Sir? Yes, I would like an ice tea, Yes Sir, curtsey.

I took a seat in the living room and a few minutes later Sabrina showed up with the ice tea. Sabrina placed the

ice tea on the table next to me and asked if she could serve me in any other way, curtsey.

Sabrina, I think that I have decided that you are too much trouble. In spite of the fact that I like to punish you, I still need to punish you too often.

Sabrina, I don't expect you to be perfect, but I guess I did think after 5 months being under my rule that you would be more pleasant to be around and I thought that I would be getting a better effort from you to please "YOUR EMPLOYER".

So, Sabrina, I am going to give you just one last chance for you to convince me that you want to be my maid. I will work with you for the rest of this year, another few weeks or so. If you are not a happy to please maid by Christmas, then I am going to fire you.

Sabrina started to open her mouth, but I cut her off and told her that she would be better off not saying anything at this time. Sabrina, for the next week I want you to come and find me every half hour and ask me every time if there is anything you can do for me, yes Sir, Curtsey, with a smile that time.

A half hour later Sabrina was back when I was in my room changing my clothes to go and work out. Sir, is there anything I can do for you? Sabrina asked. I told Sabrina to practice her curtseys 25 times, yes Sir, curtsey. As I finished getting dressed I got to enjoy watching Sabrina curtseying for me 25 times. You are dismissed, thank you Sir, curtsey.

Sabrina came and found me working out a half hour

later and curtsied and asked if she could do anything of me and I just said no, not now. Thank you, Sir, Curtsey and a smile and Sabrina left me to me work out.

I was just finishing my work out a half hour later when Sabrina came back and I told her to follow me, yes Sir, curtsey.

I had Sabrina follow me to my bedroom and I told her to wait by the bed, yes Sir, curtsey. I went in the bathroom and took off all my clothes and took a shower and went back to the bedroom naked.

I laid down on the side of the bed in the same position that Sabrina was in when I gave her that strapping. I told Sabrina to get down on her knees and give me the "kiss". Yes Sir, curtsey.

Sabrina got down on her knees and moved up between my legs and used her hands to pull me ass cheeks apart a bit and then without hesitation this time used her lips and tongue to kiss my ass hole and she did pretty well this time I thought.

Alright I said, now lick and kiss my ass cheeks a little bit. Sabrina licked and kissed all over my ass cheeks and it felt pretty good to me, I liked it. Alright Sabrina, now lick up and down on the inside of my ass crack and Sabrina did that as well and I liked it that also.

I guess Sabrina will be spending a lot more time in the future giving my ass pleasure with her mouth, I thought. You are dismissed, Sabrina got up, curtsied, and said thank you Sir and took her leave.

A half hour later Sabrina was back and this time I wanted a glass of chocolate milk, yes Sir, curtsey. Sabrina seemed to be getting the idea of polite service, but we will see if her attitude lasts. Sabrina came back with the milk and I asked me if she could serve me in any other way and I said no. Yes Sir, curtsey and Sabrina took her leave again.

When Sabrina came back again in another half hour I had her get me some more milk and some cookies as I watched some TV, yes Sir, curtsey. Sabrina came back with the milk and cookies and I told her that I did not need to see her again until 11:30, yes Sir, Curtsey. I figured that I did not need anything else that night, but that I would have Sabrina give me a nice blow job before I go to sleep.

When Sabrina came back at 11:30 she saw the big thick strap that she has felt on her ass laying on the bed next to me. I had no intention of using the strap that night, but I wanted Sabrina to see it so that she remembered to be obedient or she would be getting that strap.

Part of Sabrina's service to me was to be able to give me nice blow jobs in accordance with the blow job information I got for her over the internet and that she was suppose to read and perform accordingly.

I told Sabrina to get up on the bed with me and to give me a nice slow blow job, yes Sir, curtsey. This time Sabrina even smiled a little as she climbed up on to the bed and moved up between my thighs.

Sabrina gently grabbed my balls with her left hand and gently massaged my balls as she used her mouth

to breathe her hot breath on the tip of my cock. Then Sabrina stuck out her tongue and flicked it across my cock's head and into my cock's slit a bit and slowly licked all around the head to get my cock nice and moist.

Then she used her tongue to lick up my shaft from the bottom to the top again and again and all around the shaft to get it all wet and slippery.

Last, Sabrina took the head of my cock into her mouth and sucked on it and moved her head around in circles so that my cock head was feeling the inside of Sabrina's hot wet mouth and I could not take anymore and exploded in Sabrina's mouth.

Sabrina kept my cock in her mouth and sucked it in and out a little real slow as it lost its stiffness and only then did she let it out of her mouth while she sucked all the remaining cum off the shaft as she allowed it to escape her lips.

Sabrina must have given blow jobs to her boy friend's in the past as she seemed to know what she was doing. I know that I gave her the instructions, but it was her desire here that was different today, she sucked my cock like she wanted to this time and not because I was making her suck it.

I had no idea if Sabrina really was enjoying sucking my cock or if she was just learning that pleasing me was better than getting punished. In either case I thought, I was making progress in breaking her unfriendly spirit.

However, I was finding out over the last several months that maybe I cannot get Sabrina to be and to do as I

wish her to be and do, unless she finds that it is more acceptable to her.

I guess what I am saying is that I was hoping that if someone practiced something long enough that they would find it acceptable and maybe even enjoyable. So, I figured that if I kept training Sabrina and making her provide the same blow jobs, the same cleaning, the same curtseying, the same yes Sir, etc, that she would be begin to accept that behavior and feel that it was not so bad and become more of a routine instead of a chore.

SABRINA TRAINING DAY TWO:

Friday, after an exciting and successful first day, I was thinking about other things I could do with Sabrina that may be fun for me and maybe even challenging for her. The first thing I told Sabrina was that coming to see me every half hour seemed like too much, so make it every hour.

So over the next two hours I got an ice tea and some nice curtsies and an nice smile or two, but I did not need anything. When the Basketball game came on at 7:00 I did have Sabrina get me some snacks and some more ice tea.

When Sabrina came back I told her that I know that she knows nothing about basketball, but she needed to pick a winner anyway. She could choose the "The Heat" or New York that night. Sabrina looked at the two teams on the TV and picked the "The Heat".

Alright Sabrina, if the "The Heat" wins, you don't have to service me tomorrow. If they lose, I still get decide what you will do, Sabrina looked at me with a funny face that I had not seen before and just said, yes Sir, smiled, curtsied, and went on her way.

Sabrina had nothing to lose in this bet, only I did. If I won I would get whatever I wanted, but I get whatever I want anyway. If Sabrina won, she gets the evening off from me. So Sabrina can really only win and I can only

lose. But it made the game more exciting for me because there was a bet on it.

Sabrina came back every hour throughout the game and serviced me properly and I got some nice curtsies and even a nice smile or two. I guess that either Sabrina was getting the point that fighting me was not helping her or maybe she was just getting use to the new Boss and was accepting it, maybe both?

I was not sure and really did not care as long as she was obedient and polite and pleasant about it. I had Sabrina give me another 25 curtsies for practice, dismissed. Thank you Sir, curtsey.

Sabrina lost the bet as the THE HEAT won the game and I had Sabrina follow me to my bedroom from the living room where I was watching the game on our big 60" TV. I had her wait by the bed while I went into the bathroom and stripped naked and cleaned myself off with warm wet towel and went back and laid across the bed just like last night.

Only this time I had some cherry flavored jam with me and I told Sabrina to smear the jam all over my ass cheeks and all up and down my ass crack and even use her finger to get some inside my ass hole, yes Sir, curtsey.

Sabrina got back down on her knees and did as I told her with the cherry jam and then started first to lick it all off my ass cheeks. I told Sabrina not to just lick my ass cheeks but the use her lips to suck on them as well. Sabrina obeyed me, I also like that part.

After Sabrina cleaned my ass checks of the cherry jam she began to lick from the bottom to the top of my ass crack and cleaned all the cherry jam out of there as well.

Finally, all that was left was my ass hole and Sabina started to kiss my ass hole and French kiss it with the tongue. I then told Sabrina to stick her tongue in my asshole, to tongue fuck me and Sabrina obeyed me with only a slight hesitation.

I really thought that I was going to get to punish Sabrina again before she would tongue fuck me. However, since Sabrina did obey me I thought that maybe she was learning after all that she has no real choice in the matter if she wants to stay here and be my maid.

Sabrina did alright in trying to tongue fuck me, but my ass hole is really tight and she had trouble getting her tongue inside. Nevertheless, Sabrina, tongue fucked my ass hole pretty good. I felt really neat to have Sabrina's tongue slid in and out.

More so, I was excited by humiliating Sabrina to this degree as I knew that she had to feel that way. I was sure that tongue fucking this young rich punk was not on her list of chores that she thought she would need to be doing. Too bad for Sabrina I thought, Sabrina should have thought about that when she treated me like crap for the last 7 years.

That was very nice I told Sabrina, now back up a little while I turn over. I turned over and sat up on the end of the bed like I did yesterday and Sabrina again gave me

a nice blow job. Apparently giving me a blow job is not that hard for Sabrina, as I come so quickly.

It seems that Sabrina does not have to do very much to get me to come, maybe that was good, but I thought I would enjoy it much more if it took Sabrina longer and she had to deep throat me, at least.

SABRINA TRAINING DAY THREE:

As the game was about to start that evening I again told Sabrina to pick a team and she again picked the "The Heat". I told Sabrina that to make the bet even more interesting tonight that if I won that she would get a spanking and give me a blow job.

If she won, then I would lick her ass for her tonight. That got, at first, a frown from Sabrina, but then as she thought about it, she smiled and said, yes Sir, curtsey and went about her business.

Interesting however, that evening Sabrina came back to see if I needed anything more often than the once per hour that she was required to so. I assumed that Sabrina was just checking out the score. Now, Sabrina seemed to have a real interest in the outcome.

As well, I also did, as if the "The Heat" won, I will have to do something that I have never done before and was not even sure that I would like it. I never tried that with any of the girls I dated, or more accurately, any of girls that I fucked. But, I was willing to try it after all, Sabrina has a great ass, maybe I would like it.

Well after some late game lead changes in the score and many visits by Sabrina to see what was going on, the "The Heat" did win the game. I think that was the most exciting game I had ever watched, but I knew it really

had nothing to do with the teams, it was all about the BET!

Sabrina seemed so happy that I was even smiling for her. I had never seem Sabrina that happy about anything thru all the years she had lived here.

I was not sure if she was happy because she was not getting a spanking and did not have to eat my ass or suck my cock, or if it was because I had to eat her ass. Regardless, I was actually happy that Sabrina was happy. Since I was looking forward to trying out Sabrina's ass, this was a win, win situation for me anyway.

Alright Sabrina, since you won the bet we will go to your bedroom. I will go to the kitchen and get something and you can go and clean yourself and I will meet you in your room in a few minutes, yes Sir, curtsey.

I went to the kitchen and got some chocolate sauce as I figured that I would use that to smear over Sabrina ass cheeks and even down along her crack and into the ass hole. I enjoyed the extended service that I got from Sabrina when I had her use the cherry sauce, so it would be chocolate for me.

I got to Sabrina's room just as she was coming from the bathroom and I told her to lay over the side of the bed, yes Sir, curtsey. Sabrina laid across the side of the bed with her hips at the side of the bed and her long beautiful legs leaning down towards the floor.

I got down on my knees this time and got between Sabrina's legs and lowered her panties to her knees and then thought that we would be better off if I removed

them all together so I did. I flipped up Sabrina's short French maid dress over her ass. I start to lick her cheeks, bit them a little, suck on them some, and lick up and down Sabrina's crack.

However, with Sabrina's ass, she had all those welts from that caning I gave her a couple of days back. Feeling the welts with my tongue felt really strange. Otherwise, I still really enjoyed the view of Sabrina's ass, even with all those welts.

I stopped and got the chocolate sauce and spread it all over Sabrina's fine ass and smeared plenty in Sabrina's ass crack and used my finger to get some in her ass hole as well. I took my time licking all the sauce off of Sabrina's great looking ass as I was realizing that I loved being in this position, on my knees ,licking such a nice ass.

I licked her ass cheeks, sucked on many places and even bit her a little more but very gently. The welts however made the trip with my tongue very uneven. When I would bite Sabrina she would really squirm as I thought biting the welts most likely hurt Sabrina.

I realized that Sabrina's cheeks were cleaned of the sauce already but I was still licking and sucking and biting her. I guess I was enjoying myself more than I thought I might. Meanwhile Sabrina was moaning as if she was enjoying herself and even wiggling her ass for me a little more and I loved how that looked and felt as well.

I could not wait any longer to discover if I was going to like any of the other parts of this ass eating service and

I just dove into the crack of two of the greatest looking plump but firm ass cheeks she has ever seen.

My enthusiasm was getting the best of me I thought and slowed down. I continued to lick from the bottom to the top of Sabrina's fine ass crack. I licked along one side and then licked the other side and back again as I cleaned off all of the sauce.

After a few minutes, as the top of the crack was all cleaned of the sauce, I started to work deeper. So with every other or every third lick I licked deeper and deeper into Sabrina's crack until I was all the way in and my face was smashed between Sabrina's great ass cheeks.

These were really fine ass cheeks I thought and I was having a great time eating Sabrina's ass. I was thinking that with a bet like that I can only be the winner as this was as good as having Sabrina licking my ass I thought.

Well, I thought, the time has come to see if I like the end of this story as much as I have liked it so far. After moving my face from Sabrina's ass crack to take a breath or two. I used my hands to spread her ass cheeks a little and moved my face back into position and started to lick Sabrina's ass hole.

I licked up and down like an ice cream cone, I darted my tongue in and out and smashed my tongue against Sabrina's ass hole. I started to tongue fuck Sabrina's ass hole as well as I could and licked Sabrina's crack up and down and dove back in again. Sabrina seemed to respond well to my efforts and was moaning and

wiggling her ass in earnest while saying that's it, that's it, that's it.

I licked out all of the remaining sauce and did not miss a drop. However I was enjoying myself so much that when the sauce ran out I did not care and went to work repeating all of her previous movements only this time it was just my tongue and Sabrina's ass hole. I tongue fucked her and tongue fucker her some more.

Finally I stopped and pulled my face out of Sabrina's ass crack and took a couple of breaths and got up and said good night to Sabrina and left her room. As I was on the way out, Sabrina whispered, thank you Sir.

I was thinking as I went back to my room about how much I enjoyed that but I was concerned that I may mess up the balance of, Boss and maid, if I continued to do such things with Sabrina. On the other hand, this type of gambling on games was very exciting apparently for both of us.

So, maybe it would make Sabrina even more friendly and willing to serve me if she also got additional benefits as she obviously enjoyed that ass eating immensely. I guess we will see.

moaning as I started to fuck her real slow and I was not sure if it still hurt a little or she was enjoying it.

After all, being a guy I was never fucked in the ass and would never be fucked in the ass so I had no point of comparison. I just assumed that getting fucked in the ass was for girls and fags, not real guys like me. That assumption did not turn out well for me.

It did not take long before I climaxed in Sabrina's ass hole and filled her with cum. I withdrew and told her to go and get a hot towel and clean me off. Yes Sir, as Sabrina got up off the bed, curtseyed, and went into the bathroom and came back with a hot towel and cleaned off my cock and balls of all the left over cum and the cherry jam.

Sabrina found her panties and put them back on and actually asked if she could do anything else for me? No thank you, you are dismissed, thank you Sir, curtsey.

I took another shower and Sabrina served me some lunch and I asked her to pick her team for this afternoon's game. Sabrina again picked the "The Heat".

I told Sabrina that if I win I will give her a spanking and she will give me a nice long blow job. If she wins, she can have off tomorrow and can go shopping with my credit card.

Sabrina seemed happy with the choices based on the smile on her face. I was sure that she did not want a spanking, but the rest of the deal was way in her favor. I also think that she found this whole betting idea to be quite exciting unto itself, in spite of the downside risk

for her. I also figured that Sabrina thought she had no choice in the matter, so at least she had a shot of getting something useful for herself.

Then Sabrina surprised me when she asked permission to ask a question. Sure, what's on your mind, Sabrina? Sir, could we also add in that if I win I can get another ass licking like last night? That really surprised me, but I said sure but it goes both ways Sabrina.

I could not believe the conversation we were having over a bet. Especially considering that we never had much of any conversation ever before. Up until now it has always been me trying to dominate Sabrina and Sabrina struggling to stop me. Now, we had a conversation over a bet. I was hoping this would lead to some place good for our relationship as it was becoming not only fun but friendly also.

Just like last night, Sabrina who had no interest in basketball was in the living room much more that afternoon. Much more often than hourly when she needed to curtsey to me and ask if she could do anything for me. Sabrina seemed to be getting that part down pretty good and even seemed to have a better attitude towards her requests and curtsies.

Anyway, it seemed like Sabrina was there every 20 minutes or so to see how the game was going. I thought the game was so much more exciting than before we started to bet on the games, but Sabrina seemed to be out exciting me on this subject.

I was correct in the end as the Lakers won the game. Sabrina was really disappointed but did not seem to be

angry with me about winning the bet, almost like the thrill of the bet was enough satisfaction all by itself. Sabrina just looked at me and then lowered her head as she knew what was coming next as I told her to go and get the spanking brush and the spanking chair, yes Sir, curtsey.

I could tell she was disappointed and especially so as Sabrina had no idea how long or how hard that I would spank her. I did not give it much thought myself as I was just looking forward to spanking her nice ass of hers. However, this would be the first time I ever spanked Sabrina when she did not earn a spanking.

Sabrina came back with the spanking brush and put the spanking chair in the center of the room and just stood there next to the chair. I sat there on the couch and just watched her standing there wondering how hard and how long I was going to be spank Sabrina and wondering if the bet was now worth the risk for her.

I got up and went over and took my place on the chair. I took the brush from Sabrina's hand and pointed to my lap with it, yes Sir, curtsey and Sabrina laid over my lap. I took my time lifting her dress up over her hips so that it rested on her back as I knew it would make Sabrina all that more nervous.

I took my time lowering Sabrina's panties slowly to finally rest around her knees. I even started to pet her ass with my hand, something I had never done before. I even told Sabrina that she had a great ass and I enjoy not only spanking it, I enjoyed just looking at it, petting

it and I really enjoyed licking it for you last night, thank you sir Sabrina replied.

My heart was not into giving Sabrina a real hard spanking as it did not seem the same for me as she was not being punished, rather she was just being spanked as part of a bet. I started to spank Sabrina pretty hard but slower than usual as I watched the brush marks from each spank turn into nice shades of dark red.

Being a Sunday afternoon all the girls were out for the day and the only one home was Molly. Apparently Molly heard the spanking as I saw her lean over the railing on the second floor to see what was going on, but she quickly disappeared. Molly wanted no part of a spanking.

As I spanked Sabrina she was shooting and hollering and wiggling her nice ass all over the place but she was not crying and that was fine with me as I did not want to hurt her like I usually do when she is being punished, this was just a bunch of fun for me and part of the bet.

I spanked Sabrina with about 100 spanks, less than half of my usual spanking of Sabrina. But, I took my time so the spanking most likely lasted the same amount of time. After I stopped I just sat there and enjoyed looking at Sabrina freshly and brightly spanked ass cheeks. Then I used my hand again and petted her spanked cheeks and enjoyed not only feeling her nice ass, but how warm her cheeks were from the spanking. I could feel the welts that were still there from the caning and I could feel how Sabrina's ass was becoming swollen from the spanking. But, it was all good to me, maybe not so much for Sabrina.

I told Sabrina to get up and as she did I told her she could pull up her panties. Sabrina did so and then I told her to come to my room in about 10 minutes, yes Sir, curtsey. I also told Sabrina that she had a choice between the chocolate sauce and the cherry sauce, so choose and bring one with you, yes Sir, curtsey.

I took a shower and when I returned to the bedroom Sabrina was already there with the cherry sauce. I laid down on the side of the bed and Sabrina got down on her knees and came up between my legs and smeared the cherry sauce all over my ass cheeks, in my crack, and used her finger to get some inside my ass hole as well.

Sabrina gave me the basically the same ass eating that I got last time only different. Sabrina licked off all the cherry sauce from my ass cheeks and cleaned all the sauce out of my ass crack and also kissed on and around my ass hole like before, but different this time.

It felt to me that Sabrina was actually enjoying herself and maybe even trying to please me. Sabrina even moaned a little and used her tongue with some enthusiasm I thought. Especially when she finally tongue fucked my ass hole as it felt like she wanted me to be pleased and that she was enjoying pleasing me also.

Could it be that Sabrina was beginning to enjoy her unusual relationship with me? Regardless, after my ass eating it was time for my blow job. I again was hoping that this blow job would last longer since I already came once earlier today when I fucked Sabrina in the ass.

I told Sabrina that she needed to be more vocal with her blow jobs, for example, when you take my cock in

your mouth you need to moan and act like it is the best cock you ever tasted. You need to suck my cock like you are loving it and do more moaning as I get closer to orgasm.

When I explode in your mouth you want me to think that you cannot gobble up my cum any faster and you need to moan your way through the orgasm with great excitement.

When you are finished, you need to give me a big smile and tell me how much you enjoyed my big cock and thank me again. Understand Sabrina? Yes Sir, curtsey.

I got up on my bed and turned the TV on and got comfortable. I told Sabrina to lay between my legs and take my cock into her mouth. Now just lay there with your head on my thigh with my cock in your mouth and don't let it out at all. As time moved along I was really enjoying having my cock in Sabrina nice hot mouth keeping my cock warm.

After 10 minutes or so I told Sabrina to make me hard and without much effort on Sabrina's part she sucked me to an iron rod in no time. I told Sabrina to stop and just hold my now hard cock in her mouth. When my cock deflated all the way, I told Sabrina to get it hard again and she did.

This went on for about a half hour with Sabrina getting my cock hard and allowing it to get soft and back up again and back down again. I knew that the lesson here was for Sabrina to get use to having a cock in her mouth and in fact I was also liking having my cock in her mouth quite a bit.

I thought that it would be better for Sabrina if she too was enjoying this as that would be a bonus for Sabrina. However, I really did not care if she liked it or not, as long as she did a good job.

After the half hour was up I told Sabrina to finish the job and when I come you are to keep as much of my cum in your mouth along with my cock. So Sabrina got busy making my cock hard again and Sabrina took my cock in her mouth and started to bob her head up and down and was giving me her usual blow job, however this time she did moan like I told her.

Sabrina's moaning seemed to excite me even more than usual. Sabrina seemed to understand that and became more aggressive in her cock sucking and moaned even more and louder and in no time had me spewing my cum all over the inside of her mouth.

For the next 10 minutes or so, I had Sabrina just lay her head on my thigh again and hold my cock and a lot of my cum in her mouth until her digestive juices dissolved the cum and she had to naturally swallow it.

This exercise took about 45 minutes and then I told Sabrina she could finish up. Sabrina sucked any remaining cum off my cock as she allowed it to withdraw from her mouth. Sabrina looked up at me and with a big smile on her face told me that that was delicious, you have a great cock Sir, and thank you very much for letting me suck it for you.

SABRINA TRAINING DAY FIVE: MONDAY

There was no game on Monday night and not much else happened on Monday. However, Sabrina had to keep coming and seeing me and asking if she could do anything for me. One time I told her no and she would say thank you Sir, curtsey, and go back to work.

Another time I would make Sabrina practice her curtsies 25 times before dismissing her. Another time I was just getting out of the shower so I had her give me the kiss of submission. I always seemed to like Sabrina's nice full lips all over my ass cheeks and ass hole as she would kiss them for a minute or so.

This one time Sabrina stopped by to ask if she could get me anything, I said sure Sabrina. Let's take a tour of the house and see how you housework is looking these days. Sabrina all of a sudden got this real nervous look on her face.

I suppose she thought that I was not going to happy with her cleaning. I thought that was strange as after all, cleaning, was Sabrina's main job, sucking my cock and getting it in the ass are just bonuses for me.

Nevertheless, we walked around the house and looked in many rooms. but not all of them. I especially paid attention to the bathrooms and the tile as that was one area that Sabrina never paid much attention to in the

past and was one of the main reasons that Sabrina had been punished in the past.

To my surprise and I think Sabrina's as well, I thought that everything was looking pretty good. I looked at Sabrina and asked her if I should look in her bathroom? Sabrina, looked at me and asked if I could please wait until tomorrow night, Curtsey?

I just smiled and thought that as Sabrina seemed to be improving in every area, that I would not go out of my way to find a reason to punish her, but I thought that she got the message that surprise inspection would be part of her future. So, I told Sabrina, sure, tomorrow night will be fine. Thank you Sir, curtsey and this time with a big smile.

When I was ready for bed I told Sabrina to get on the bed with me and keep my cock in her mouth for the entire 30 minutes the news was on. She was not suppose to get me to cum, but she was suppose to keep me hard the whole time.

For the most part she did not have to do anything but keep my cock in her mouth as that was all it took to keep it hard. But, I thought that it was good practice for Sabrina to get use to having a cock in her mouth so she would learn to enjoy it and look forward to it in the future

Funny what I thought of at times like these. I was thinking that all girls should learn how to give good blow jobs but it seemed like a hard thing to learn. You know, getting that big thing in your mouth and down your throat.

Meanwhile, guys, yes except for the fags, don't have to learn much at all. I mean, I have not learned how to eat a pussy and that does not seem to stop me from getting to fuck any girl I want. I have no interest in sticking my face in any girls pussy. YUK, pussies are all swishy and gooey, why bother?

SABRINA TRANING DAY SIX: TUESDAY

I was thinking about the bets and thought that I was being too generous with me eating out Sabrina's ass for her. I did enjoy it but thought that it may ruin the Boss, submissive dynamic, if the fun was going two ways.

I did not mind allowing Sabrina to go shopping as part of a bet, but I was thinking that I should not be servicing her sexually in any way. I also did not want to spank her as part of a bet as I did not enjoy it that much as she was not being punished.

I really love to spank Sabrina when she is disobedient or disrespectful, or does not clean well. Then I want to punish her, then I want to hurt her. But, just for fun, did not turn out to be much fun.

I also figured that having Sabrina eating my ass or sucking my cock was nothing to bet about as I want her to do those things anyway whenever I tell her to.

So I redesigned the winning and losing side of the bets to things that would not usually happen otherwise. So this night, if I won, I would get a massage from Sabrina. If Sabrina won, she would not have to give me any sexual service and could go shopping the next day.

This way, if I lose then I lose my blow job for the evening and have to pay for her shopping trip. If Sabrina loses

she just has to give me a massage. I would still get my ass service and blow job.

This evening Sabrina stuck with the "The Heat" and won the bet, so I got no service that evening and I gave Sabrina my credit card and told her that she could spend up to $1000.00 for anything she wanted. Sabrina gave me a big smile and even thanked me, curtsey, even though she did not need to do so under the circumstances.

SABRINA TRAINING DAY SIX: WEDNESDAY:

Wednesday nights bet was that Sabrina could have three days off and no sexual service that evening. If I won I still got my sexual services and a massage. The "The Heat" lost that night and Sabrina gave me a surprisingly good massage.

I guess I was surprised as massaging was not something Sabrina was trained to do. Sabrina also did not hurry like she hated the whole thing and she made me feel like she wanted to do a nice job and make it feel good for me.

After my shower I had Sabrina lay over the side of the bed and I fucked her real good in the ass. However, that night in an effort to make it last longer I fucked her real slow and kept stopping when I thought I was going to cum. I loved fucking Sabrina in the ass, mostly because I loved Sabrina's ass. Sabrina had one of the nicest ass's a guy could hope for.

Sabrina had a nicer ass then any of the 12 girls I fucked in the last 12 weeks. Yes, I know 12 girls in 12 weeks, I did like to fuck a new girl every week, but it was cutting in on my tennis time, so I may cut back to only 2 or 3 new girls each month.

Sabrina's ass was somewhat muscular and higher up and down then plump sideways. So Sabrina had a longer ass crack then, say, Ally who had more of a box type ass,

which is more square. Ally's was plumper side to side and less muscular.

I finally started to fuck Sabrina real hard and I think she liked my balls slapping again her pussy and she was squirming and moaning like she was having a good time, at least I thought so. I exploded inside Sabrina's ass and went to clean myself off and came back with a warm towel and cleaned Sabrina's ass as well and dried her off.

I was thinking that maybe I was getting too nice to Sabrina but the relationship was starting to work as she was becoming completely obedient and even acted like she was not hating her position any more. So, I thought I could be nice and still be very stern and strict with Sabrina, it seemed to be working.

I laid down on the bed to watch the news and had Sabrina get between my legs again like last night. However, last night I just had Sabrina hold my cock in her mouth for most of the 30 minutes the news was on, even though I had a limp cock.

This night, however, I made Sabrina try and keep my cock hard, which was not all that easy in the beginning as I just had a orgasm in Sabrina's ass. So, Sabrina had to work at it a little bit, but she managed to keep it hard almost for the whole thirty minutes.

However, that was the easy part as I also made Sabrina keep my entire cock in her mouth, which meant that my cock was in her throat when it was the hardest and that was much more difficult for Sabrina. I guess Sabrina was lucky that I have a short cock, only about 5 inches long,

but somewhat fatter then a lot of the other guys that I saw at the gym.

So, Sabrina would get my cock hard and have to hold it all the way in her mouth so that her nose was touching my belly and then as it would deflate she could relax more and more as it would go back down and then she needed to start all over again.

When the news was over I told Sabrina to finish me and she was actually able to deep throat me very easily after all that practice and was able to give me a nice deep blow job and I happily filled her mouth with cum in under two minutes.

Sabrina was really getting the hang of cock sucking. But, I could not tell if she was doing so just to avoid more punishment or if she was enjoying herself. I never did ask and in a way I did not care all that much as long as she sucked my cock well. But, I was curious.

SABRINA TRAINING DAY SEVEN: THURSDAY.

The bet for tonight's game was that if Sabrina won, she would get three days off and provide no sexual services this evening.

If I won, I would get another massage.

Sabrina asked permission to ask a question, curtsey? Yes Sabrina, go ahead I said. Sabrina surprised me with her question which was if she won could she take me in the ass with a strap on?

I looked at Sabrina and thought about why she would even have a strap on, but otherwise I thought about it and told her no! Guys don't take it in the ass, that's just for girls. Yes Sir, curtsey.

Damn if the "The Heat" did not win again and Sabrina got three days off. I still had Ally and Cally to handle the maid work so that was alright and Sabrina deserved a few days off anyway as she has been very good and obedient.

After Sabrina's 7 days of obedience practice, she seemed much more comfortable to be around. I never thought that would be the case as I assumed that I was getting rid of her after the new year, But who knows now, maybe it will work out?

MORE ABOUT ME:

Closing in on Christmas this year, I started to get another group of kids that no longer liked me. At this time it was the biggest group and growing almost every week.

You see, ever since I had my first sexual relation a little more than 3 months ago all I was interested in doing with the girls was fucking them. Now, I suppose that would be normal for a guy my age, but most of the other guys would have sex with the same girl over and over again. Most of the guys could not get very many girls to have sex with them.

However, I did not seem interested in any of the girls as in a relationship, I looked at the girls as my own personal pool of "fuckies" You know, those who I have fucked and those who I have not fucked yet, but intended to fuck later. After all, one guy cannot fuck them all in only three mouths, there were so many and it takes time to get to them all.

Mt Sister told me that I was getting a real reputation of a "fuck them and forget them" guy. I did not seem to care as I did not have any interest in really dating any of them for any period of time. I just thought it was a

challenge to get them to have sex with me and then I was finished with them.

As time went on I thought that if so many of the girls were finding out from the other girls that I had a small penis and that together with my growing reputation may cause me to have more trouble attracting my next "fuckie".

Considering that I could get all the blow jobs I wanted from Sabrina and considering that I could fuck Sabrina in the ass all I wanted, I was not finding the lack of girl friends to be a problem. Being able to use Sabrina was actually easier and more fun for me.

Now, I also named a new group, "The three Lesbos". There were these three girls that always hung around together and everyone would say that they were lesbians. So, to me the name fit and with the other names I provided over the past four months, it was a big hit. Yes, I know, maybe not a big hit for the Lesbos.

So, now we can add those three to the list of kids who don't like me anymore, as well as, all the Lesbos who were not part of that trio, as they stay hidden in the background.

To my surprise, Cally and I were playing chess one day and she asked me about the Lesbos name? Cally's position was that it was just not nice to be labeling people like that, that is something that only bad boys do and you Mort have been one of the good guys.

I did not defend myself to Cally, after all, who is she to question me? I just maintained it was all in fun and it

was true, so what? Cally told me that she knows about "The three blackies", "The three fags", and "The three fatties". Now, Mort, "The three Lesbos". That's bad boy behavior, Mort, you are better than that.

I sort of ended the conversation by ignoring Cally and changing the subject to Christmas, the following week. So, we spoke about Christmas presents and how Cally's past Christmas's went when she had a father and now that she did not have a father. But, at least I got Cally off the bad boy stuff.

CHRISTMAS:

This was the first Christmas that Molly had any money to buy her two girls anything nice. In the past Molly was just able to feed them and keep a roof over their heads. However, since Molly moved in here with Mindy and me, she has had no food or shelter expenses, as we let them live with us for free.

Mindy and I never asked them for anything from molly, so Molly's money was all hers. The only expenses Molly had was for auto expenses and clothes. So, Molly was able to save some money for the first time in the last five years.

Molly and I had a long discussion as to what to get Ally and Cally for Christmas. I was willing to buy them some things, especially Cally, as she has been very nice to live with and I thought that she should be rewarded for making the adjustments, although we have yet to see her second report card which was coming out after the new year.

Molly was concerned that if I spent money on the girls, it would dwarf what she could afford and make her gifts less impactful, in her mind. I could not disagree with Molly, so I actually gave Molly the money to buy them each a computer and a cell phone. I thought those gifts

would help them in school and help Molly keep tract of them as well.

The fact that Ally and Cally would think that all the gifts came from their mother was fine with me, I was not looking for the credit. I also did not care to buy anything for Ally anyway, only Cally, so that solved my problem as well.

We all had a nice Christmas morning opening the presents, especially Ally and Cally who both got a lot of nice clothes for the first time in their lives. The cell phones and the computers were also a big hit.

I could not have been happier for the two of them as their lives were slowly turning around for the better.

Sabrina, well, Sabrina has been doing very well since our week long training session. So, Mindy and I bought her two computers. One for her and one for her mother back in South America. That way they could email one another and or Skype if that wanted. Mindy also bought Sabrina some nice clothes for when she want out.

Sabrina was also treated as part of the family for the entire day and although she helped Molly with making and serving and cleaning up after dinner, I did not make her wear her French maid outfit.

We all had another real nice dinner that Molly cooked and all the girls helped out doing something, even Ally this time.

For Mindy and me, we were happy to bring some joy to the others, but later we had a private conversation

about how much we missed our parents and that resulted in both of us having a good cry together as we sure missed our parents, this was our first Christmas without them!

REPORT CARD NUMBER TWO:

It was early January 2006 and it was report card day again. My sister Mindy got three "B"s and two "A"S. I got four "A"s and only one "B" again.

I told Ally and Cally to meet me in the living room after dinner at 6:30 pm with their report cards. I let Molly and my sister know in case they wanted to be there. I expected to see Molly there, after all, they were her kids. Molly did show up as well as my sister.

Mindy, Molly, and me were sitting on the couch when the two girls showed up on time. Cally did not have any facial expression that would indicate that she was worried at all. Ally, well, she looked real nervous, so I guess we know who was getting another spanking.

I thought we would take the easy path first and I held out my hand for Cally to give me her report card. Cally, to my great surprise and to her mother's great surprise did not just pass all of her subjects, she got all "B"s, not even one "C".

Molly was especially thrilled as Cally never got marks that high before. I told Cally that we were so happy with her report card and we would give her something extra special for her effort, but first we would deal with Ally.

Cally gave me a big special smile that made me smile as well. Cally's smile just seemed to light up the room.

I held out my hand and in a manner of disrespect Ally sort of shoved her report card into my hand while smashing it. I looked at Ally and she just gave me her meanest face. I thought that Ally was just not to smart as she was trying to anger the guy who was going to be spanking her in a few minutes.

I mean, was she telling me that she wanted me to be angry and punish her even more severely? I did not think so, I just thought that Ally was not bright enough to overcome her emotions in favor of protecting herself from a harsher punishment.

Ally got two "D"s this time and three "C"s. While that was a big improvement it still meant that she needed to get those two "D"s up to almost "B"s by the end of the school year to not get left behind.

Keep in mind that Catholic schools are not like public schools they don't practice "no child left behind" they actually expect you to learn something and don't pass everyone just so they can brag that everyone passed.

Anyway, apparently the simple spanking that I gave to Cally for her last report card was enough to get her attention. Apparently, Cally did not any more of my spanking brush and the embarrassment of having her panties taken down in front of everyone and crying her eyes out while having her bare bottom spanked.

Apparently, Cally, did not want to stand in the corner while showing off her brightly spanked ass cheeks.

But, more importantly to me, Cally proved that what I thought about her was true and she was much smarter than her grades showed.

Conversely that hard strapping that I gave Ally got did not affect her attitude well enough for her to do that much better in school. So I need to think of a better plan, after all, we only had a half a year left to get her average grades to passing level.

I told everyone that we needed to go down to the basement for Ally's punishment and we all got up and went down to the basement. I told Ally to lay over the punishment bench and as she looked at her mother for help, Ally saw none coming and laid down on the bench.

I put wrist and ankle cuffs on Ally and then hooked her wrist and ankles real tight to the legs of the bench. I also put a thick leather strap around her waist to hold her even tighter to the bench.

I went to the cabinet and took out a cane. This is the first time anyone other than Sabrina has seen the cane so they did not know what to expect. I took the cane over to Ally's face and showed it to her and told her that this cane is going to make her real sorry she did not get better marks and this will just be the beginning of your punishment.

I walked around behind Ally and flipped her skirt up over her waist and then pulled her panties down to her knees. This position left her ass slightly rounded but sticking out to provide a nice target for my cane as it did with Sabrina when I gave her a good caning.

Also, in this position, just like with Sabrina's ass Ally's ass is in just the right position for me to fuck her in the ass or to go around to her face and get a blow job. However, as much as I was thinking about how much fun that could be, I also knew that I could not expect to do either of those two things with Ally.

I swished the cane in the air a few times and then SWISH! The cane landed across both ass cheeks and wrapped around Ally's left ass cheek and finished on the side of her ass where there is no plumpness to protect her. WOW! Cally said, look at that mark.

I am sure that Ally wanted to be brave this time like she has in the past and not show any reaction except to moan a little. However, unlike with the strapping I gave Ally, Ally was not able to hold her reaction at all this time and she wiggled her ass real nice for me and moaned loudly and moaned for a long time as it seemed that as the cane mark was developing the pain was getting worse.

SWISH! And I got another big struggle from Ally, I loved how she wiggled her ass when I was strapping her and now I get the same thrill with the cane, just like with Sabrina. SWISH! SWISH! SWISH! And Ally had five nice welts growing before my eyes. I gave her five more SWISHES!

Within a minute Ally started to cry and scream a whole lot. Ally screamed so loud and cried so hard she was showing me that she was in so much pain that she could no longer control herself. If Ally had any thoughts about

showing me that I was not winning this mental battle with her, it appeared to be gone.

SWISH! SWISH! SWISH! SWISH! SWISH! Now I certainly had Ally's attention as she is in real pain now, as there was no fight left in her as she was freely crying her heart out and screaming with each SWISH! After the first dozen I stopped.

I walked around to Ally's right side instead of her left side and SWISH! SWISH! SWISH! SWISH! SWISH! I was loving beating Ally, just like I loved beating Sabrina with this cane as I was loving how all the welt marks were developing on Ally's ass cheeks and I was loving watching that real nice ass of Ally's wiggle all over in pain, and I was loving listening to Ally scream and cry her eyes out.

SWISH! SWISH! SWISH! SWISH! SWISH! Just as with Sabrina, I was having so much fun I gave Ally two more extra hard SWISH! and SWISH! just to listen to Ally scream extra loud and listen to her enhanced crying, I was having a great time. I gave Ally 24 hard SWISHES! and she had 24 nice dark red and purple welts across her ass cheeks, 12 welts on each side of her ass.

I walked around to Ally's face and watched her cry for a minute or so. Just watching Ally cry and cry and cry was a thrill all by itself, the same thrill I got from hurting Sabrina with this cane. I waited until she calmed down a bit and asked her if she was ready to obey me now?

Yes Sir, Ally managed to get out between the tears and gasping for air as her nose was clogged with snot. So, Ally, are you going to get better marks starting tomorrow?

Yes Sir. Well, Ally, I would like to believe you but I think you need some more encouragement first.

I walked back around behind Ally and SWISH! SWISH! SWISH! SWISH! SWISH! SWISH! SWISH! SWISH! SWISH! SWISH! 10 more hard welt causing and pain screaming welts were delivered without as much time in between for Ally to adjust to them causing even a more intense pain.

Ally was not even finished screaming from one SWISH! before the next SWISH! hit her and she was having a problem breathing with her snot fill nose while trying to scream and cry and breath all at the same time. I gave Ally two more SWISH! SWISH! from that side and walked around to her other side.

SWISH! SWISH! SWISH! SWISH! SWISH! SWISH! SWISH! SWISH! SWISH! SWISH! SWISH! I put the cane down and Ally was just one big mess of crying and screaming and moaning and trying to breath.

Ally's ass was covered with 25 welts from the left side and 25 welts from the right side. So the center of Ally's ass was nothing but welts. Both sides of Ally's ass had 25 individual welts that looked real angry and real painful.

I hit Ally extra hard with that cane that day for a few reasons. First, to be truthful, I wanted her to do better in school and thought that this was the only way of getting Ally's attention.

However, I also enjoyed punishing Ally. I enjoyed punishing Ally a whole lot and I was very thankful Ally

gave me the reason to beat her like that. I spanked Cally twice and it was not as much fun for me as Cally was more submissive and I could not punish her that hard as she was not that bad of a kid.

But with Ally, I think beating her was almost as much fun as beating Sabrina, except that I could not fuck Ally in the ass like I could with Sabrina. Maybe next year when she is 18 I would fuck Ally in the ass as well and get her to suck my cock too.

Regardless, my underwear was wet from pre cum dripping due to my intense excitement in caning Ally like that. If I could have had an orgasm without any physical stimulation, this would have been the time I thought. I left Ally there on the bench as she was still crying and crying very hard.

I knew that ass of hers was going to be sore and hurting for some time and I liked it, I just loved my new job as the Boss, The disciplinarian, the one with all the power, this was great, just great I thought.

I put the cane back and waited another minute before unhooking Ally and told her to go back and stand in the corner. Cally, you will come back to the living room with us and we will discuss you prize for good marks.

As well, we will also discuss Ally's additional punishment for her continued bad marks. I heard a small moan from Ally when she heard that part of the announcement and I thought that was a good sign as it showed fear of the additional punishment. After all, that is what punishment was all about, making one afraid of getting punished so they avoid getting punished.

We all went back to the living room and Ally went up to the top of the stairs where we could all see her and she took her place standing in the corner. Ally was a little unsteady on her feet but managed to get into the correct position while holding up the back of her skirt so she had her well welted ass on full display.

I told everyone that, in life, there are rewards and punishments for all most everything we do in life. Ally was an example of one who choose to make the wrong decisions over and over again and so she continues to experience punishment and will do so until she learns to behave and make better decisions.

Cally on the other hand has only been spanked twice in the past six months and Cally has not repeated any of her bad decisions. So, I believe that Cally should be rewarded for her good behavior, for being pleasure to live with, and now her good marks in school, for being such a good girl.

Therefore, I have decided to lease Cally a new car as her present for her accomplishments. I will let Cally pick out any car she wants up to $50,000.00 in price. I almost cried myself as Cally started to cry.

However, this time Cally tears were from happiness not pain like Ally's tears were. Cally was so happy and I was so happy for her. I was so thrilled to be able to do this for Cally.

This is the first time I had ever experienced such a thrill for being generous to someone. To be honest, I think it felt better then the thrill I get punishing Sabrina or Ally.

The thrill of bringing happiness to another, interesting, I thought.

Meanwhile, Ally burst into tears, tears of jealously and I was sure more disgust for me for treating Cally so well and her so poorly. Ally cried and cried and cried so hard that you would have thought I was beating her again.

However, I continued, Cally, there are rules for having a car. You do not drink, you do not take drugs, you are home by midnight every night, you continue to get good marks in school, and last Cally, you are not allowed to drive your sister Ally to or from school, nor is she ever allowed to drive your car.

No Cally, Ally needs to continue to take the bus until her marks improve. Understand the rules Cally? Yes Sir, and Cally gave me a big smile and then came over and gave me a hug too. Both Cally and I had tears dripping down our faces as we hugged.

I could understand the tears for Cally, after all she is a girl. However, I should not have any tears myself as I am almost a man and men don't cry. Yet, I had tears of happiness for Cally and they did not feel like a bad thing to me.

I looked over to Molly and both Molly and Mindy also had tears dripping down their faces. So, I guess I was doing the right thing for a change. After all, all I have heard lately is that I am becoming a bad boy.

Alright, now that we are finished with the good news for Cally, let's have Ally come down and share her additional

bad news with her. Ally, I called to her, come on down here.

When Ally arrived she did not want to look at me as she just looked at the floor. I told her to go and get Sabrina and to come back. What are you going to do my sister asked? You'll see, Mindy.

Ally came right back with Sabrina, yes Sir, curtsey? Sabrina, beginning right now Ally will be your maid assistant. You will dress her the way you dress and teach her to behave as you are suppose to behave, including the proper attitude and curtseying.

Ally, you will become Sabrina's assistant and you will clean whatever she tells you to clean, whenever she tells you to clean it, and you will behave the way Sabrina teaches you to behave. If you don't want to learn anything in school, then you will need a backup trade and in this case that will be a life as a maid, so you may as learn now to be a maid now.

Sabrina, now you are in charge of Ally. If she does not behave properly or does not obey you without question, then you need to let me know that she needs to be punished. If you fail to let me know and I find out that you were too easy with her, then I will punish both of you. Understand Sabrina? yes Sir, curtsey.

Good Sabrina, now you can have Ally's help all day on Saturdays and Sundays and every day after school after she finishes her homework, until further notice. Ally, before you say anything else to get yourself in more trouble, yes, this means that you are grounded until your marks improve. In fact, let's say that to get

ungrounded, you need to bring me passing test marks in every subject.

Then we will revise you maid schedule based on how good the marks are at that time. But, until then, Ally, you go to school, you will do your homework, and you are Sabrina's maid assistant. You will not watch TV Before 10 pm and you will not use your computer or phone before 10 pm as you will be on duty. Understand Ally? Yes Sir, Ally whispered at me as she faced the floor.

One last thing Sabrina, you need to teach Ally to behave quickly because as of Monday afternoon, I will expect perfection from her. Yes Sir, curtsey.

Alright Ally, you can return to the corner and when the timer goes off you can report to Sabrina to begin being her assistant. Mindy looked at me and said, very interesting, but maybe a good idea.

Molly told me that she thought that the caning was really harsh, but maybe Ally needed to be treated that harshly as nothing else has worked so far. Molly also said that the maid idea was interesting and may even be a good idea.

This is the end of the first book as you are up to date on my life thru the first Five months or so of my new life with Molly, Ally, Cally, and the new Sabrina, the French maid Sabrina.

Over all I have had a great time being the Boss of the house and the king of my school. Other then the fact that my parents are gone and that miss them, life could not be better for me.

I have learned that it is very exciting to Boss others around, to embarrass and humiliate others, and to punish others as well.

Yes, I know that it may not be much fun for them, but then I really just did not care as I was having a great time.

My next book, THE BAD BOY AND HIS FRENCH MAIDS, TWO, the second book in the series, will be out shortly and will begin with Ally's maid training over the next seven days. Ally turned out to be a lot of fun to train, humiliate, and punish then I first thought.

Ally looked so sexy in her French maid outfit that I would get erections all the time just looking at her. My

cock really liked what it saw. Especially when Ally had to curtsey to me and I knew that was humiliating her to no end.

Anyway, after Ally is finished being trained, I have included many of the other fun things and adventures I had over the next six months or so with my new house mates.

I think everyone will enjoy the transformation with Cally as she continues to surprise me almost every time she opens her mouth.

There was still two more report cards to come out this year. Will Cally keep up her marks and keep the car, or lose her car and get another spanking?

Will Ally ever pass all her classes or will Ally continue to be my second French maid and continue to get herself into trouble?

Will I continue down the path to being a "BAD BOY" as I have been told now by Molly, Cally, and Mindy?

Later, the summer vacation brings a few surprises, one I could not believe and I don't think you will either, but it really happened. It was a great summer for me, the best of my life, Bad Boy and all.

The Bad Boy and his French Maids

A sissy maid missy bad boy series, part one

The Bad Boy and his French Maids, Two

A sissy maid missy bad boy series, part two

The Bad Boy and his French Maids, Three

A sissy maid missy bad boy series, part three

The Bad Boy Gets Punished

A sissy maid missy bad boy series, part four

The Bad Boy Gets Punished, Two

A sissy maid missy bad boy series, part five

The Bad Boy, The Sissy Maid

> A sissy maid missy bad boy series, part six

The Bad Boy, the sissy Maid, Two

> A sissy maid missy bad boy series, part seven

The Bad Boy, the Sissy Maid, Three

> A sissy maid missy bad boy series, part eight

The Bad Boy, The Sissy Maid, Four

> A sissy maid missy bad boy series, part nine

The Bad Boy, The Sissy Maid, Five

> A sissy maid missy bad boy series, part Ten

> A sissy maid missy bad boy series, continues.